SAMANTHA SANDERSON

AT THE
MOVIES

faiThGirLz!

SAMANTHA SANDERSON

AT THE MOVIES

BOOK ONE

BY ROBIN CAROLL

For Remington …
Because you're smart and funny and beautiful and
you inspire me.
Every.
Single.
Day.
I love you. ~ Mom

Also by Robin Caroll
Samantha Sanderson On the Scene

Other books in the growing Faithgirlz!™ library

Bibles
The Faithgirlz! Bible
NIV *Faithgirlz! Backpack Bible*

Faithgirlz! Bible Studies
Secret Power of Love
Secret Power of Joy
Secret Power of Goodness
Secret Power of Grace

Fiction
The Good News Shoes
Riley Mae and the Rock Shocker Trek
Riley Mae and the Ready Eddy Rapids

From Sadie's Sketchbook
Shades of Truth (Book One)
Flickering Hope (Book Two)
Waves of Light (Book Three)
Brilliant Hues (Book Four)

Sophie's World Series
Meet Sophie (Book One)
Sophie Steps Up (Book Two)
Sophie and Friends (Book Three)
Sophie's Friendship Fiasco (Book Four)
Sophie Flakes Out (Book Five)
Sophie's Drama (Book Six)

The Lucy Series
Lucy Doesn't Wear Pink (Book One)
Lucy Out of Bounds (Book Two)

Lucy's Perfect Summer (Book Three)
Lucy Finds Her Way (Book Four)

The Girls of Harbor View
Girl Power (Book One)
Take Charge (Book Two)
Raising Faith (Book Three)
Secret Admirer (Book Four)

Boarding School Mysteries
Vanished (Book One)
Betrayed (Book Two)
Burned (Book Three)
Poisoned (Book Four)

Nonfiction
Faithgirlz Handbook
Faithgirlz Journal
Food, Faith, and Fun! Faithgirlz Cookbook
Real Girls of the Bible
My Beautiful Daughter
You! A Christian Girl's Guide to Growing Up
Girl Politics
Everybody Tells Me to Be Myself, but I Don't Know Who I Am

Devotions for Girls Series
No Boys Allowed
What's a Girl to Do?
Girlz Rock
Chick Chat
Shine On, Girl!
Check out www.faithgirlz.com

ZONDERKIDZ

Samantha Sanderson At the Movies
Copyright © 2014 by Robin Caroll Miller

This title is also available as a Zondervan ebook.
Visit www.zondervan.com/ebooks

Requests for information should be addressed to:

Zonderkidz, 3900 Sparks Drive, Grand Rapids, Michigan 49546

ISBN 978-0-310-74245-6

Editor: Kim Childress
Art direction: Deborah Washburn
Cover design: Cindy Davis
Cover illustration: Jake Parker
Interior design: Ben Fetterley

Printed in the United States of America

14 15 16 17 18 19 /DCI/ 20 19 18 17 16 15 14 13 12 11 10 9 8 7 6 5 4 3 2 1

CHAPTER 1

SATURDAY NIGHT AT THE MOVIES

There was just something right about popcorn so covered in butter that you had to lick your fingers.

Samantha "Sam" Sanderson swiped her hands over her jeans and reached for her drink in the dark theater.

Her best friend sitting beside her did the same. Makayla shoved the straw in her mouth.

Slurp!

Sam and Makayla stared at one another by the light from the movie, then giggled before they shushed themselves.

"I need more to drink," whispered Makayla.

"You think?" Sam whispered back.

"Let's go to the concession stand."

Sam stared at the big screen where the hero fought

the villain to have justice prevail. Problem was, she'd figured out who the bad guy was well before the movie revealed him as the killer.

"Come on." Makayla stood and inched down the row.

Sam stood and followed. Not that there were a lot of people to scoot by. To celebrate the start of the school year, Sam's dad had agreed to take the girls to see the late movie. There weren't many people in attendance. Could be because of the recent controversy about the theater closing to the public tomorrow for a special, private viewing of the new faith-based movie, *Faithfully HIS*. Area churches had come together to rent the entire theater. Pretty cool, in Sam's opinion. Others didn't agree.

They made their way to the center stairs and headed down. Sam stopped at the last row and ducked her head next to the man sitting in the aisle seat. "Dad, we're running to the concession stand to get a refill. Be right back."

"Okay," he whispered back with a nod.

She shook her head as she followed Makayla toward the exit. If the place had been as busy as it usually was on a Saturday night, she'd have texted her father about where they were going. No way would he have let her and Makayla go into the lobby alone if the theater was packed. Guess it was all a blessing.

"I have to go to the bathroom first," Makayla said as they stepped into the hall.

Sam blinked against the lights that seemed entirely

too bright until they turned the corner into the ladies' room. The light in the entry seemed to have burned out. As they turned, she noticed a sliver of light sneaking out from under the supply closet door. Talk about a waste of electricity. She tried the knob — it was locked.

Makayla skipped down to a stall while Sam stood in front of the sinks. The water automatically spewed from the spout as she extended her hands. Might take super-powered soap to get all the butter residue off her hands.

"I can't believe how tired I am." Makayla joined her at the sink, fighting a yawn.

Immediately, Sam yawned. "Stop that. It's only ten forty."

"Yeah, the movie should be over in a few minutes."

"No surprise how it'll end." Sam waved her hand in front of the hand towel dispenser. A paper towel shot out from the machine.

"But that's what makes it good. We know they'll live happily ever after." Makayla snatched the towel before Sam could.

"Really?" Sam grinned and waved her hand again. "What if there's a car accident?"

Makayla frowned. "That's morbid. Why do you do that? Normal people don't think like that."

Sam shrugged, still grinning, and tossed her wadded towel into the trashcan. "What can I say? I think outside the box."

"You're a freak against nature." Makayla threw her used paper towel into the trash.

"Force of nature, Mac. Force of nature."

"Hey, did you get that text from Nikki about the pool party next weekend?"

"Seriously?"

"At three next Saturday. Her house."

"No." Of course not. Nikki Cole was Aubrey Damas's best friend, and Aubrey hated Sam. No way would either of them ever invite her to anything. They normally didn't include Makayla either. "Since when did you and Nikki become such good friends?"

"We aren't. The invite surprised me, so I wondered if she sent out a mass text to everybody."

Sam whipped out her iPhone and checked her inbox. Sure enough, there was a message waiting. She pressed the screen to open her unread message. Maybe this year would be different. Maybe whatever problem Aubrey had with Sam had disappeared. Maybe...

Her hopes free-fell to her toes. The text was from her father.

"Dad says the movie's about over. He'll meet us in the lobby," Sam told her best friend.

"Oh, we'd better hurry. I want to get a drink before everyone comes out." Makayla headed out of the ladies room.

Sam shook her head. Her best friend had a one-track mind.

She trailed behind Makayla to the lobby, waiting while her friend grabbed a soda. Seconds later, the theater door opened and people flooded the lobby. A few stood in line in front of the one open register at the concession stand, but most filtered their way to the main exit. Dad joined them almost immediately.

"Did you girls enjoy the movie?"

"Yes, sir. Thank you for bringing me." Makayla smiled.

Someone brushed against her arm, jarring her. The cup slipped from her fingers, exploding onto the floor. Soda splashed everywhere.

Makayla's face turned redder than the fiery banner of the IMAX logo. "I'm sorry." She stooped and picked up the fallen cup. "I'm so sorry, Mr. Sanderson. Your slacks are soaked."

"Don't worry about it." Dad glanced around. "I'll go find someone to get a mop. You girls stay here. We don't want someone slipping and falling."

"I'm so sorry," Makayla told Sam.

"Stop it, Mac. It was an accident. No big deal. Clothes wash." The last thing Sam needed was for Makayla to start bawling. She hated tears. "Go throw the cup in the trash. Dad's got someone headed this way."

The girl Dad led toward them had a roll of paper towels in her hand with a plastic bag. Seriously? Sam glanced at the pool of soda on the floor. Even if the girl got all the moisture up, it would still be sticky.

Dad must have been having the same argument with

the employee as he waved at the spill. "See? You need a mop."

"Sir, I've called my manager. She has to unlock the supply closet since we've already gone through the shutdown process for the night." The girl unwound paper towels and crouched as she sopped up the soda.

Makayla grabbed a handful of the towels and swiped.

That reminded Sam ... "You might mention to her that somebody left the light on in the supply room by the ladies' restroom."

The girl slipped the drenched towels into the plastic trash bag. "Which side of the theater?"

Sam pointed to the side they'd just left.

"No one's been in that supply closet tonight."

"I dunno." Sam shrugged. "I'm just saying the light was on."

A woman in the theater's logoed shirt appeared behind them. "Well, this is quite the mess."

"I'm sorry. Someone hit my arm and the cup fell." Makayla's voice cracked as she stared up at the woman.

"It was an accident. Not your fault." Dad met the manager's stare. "But obviously, a mop is required."

"And this girl says the supply closet by theater six has the light on." The girl wiped the floor with a bit more energy since her manager arrived.

"I'll show you." Sam didn't wait for a response as she led the way to the bathroom. She didn't want to get left cleaning the floor. Gross.

Dad and the manager followed on her heels, Dad's shoes squeaking on the floor. She reached the door. Light spilled from under the door. "See?" She pointed.

The manager selected a key from her large ring holding about twenty keys, and unlocked the door. She rolled out the mop bucket and the mop, reached for the light switch, then stopped.

"What's that?" she mumbled under her breath as she reached for a cardboard box sitting on the floor. It'd been partially hidden by the mop bucket. She used a key to rip up the tape holding the box closed, then pulled back a flap. She gasped and took a step backward. "Is this some kind of a joke?"

Dad pulled her from the closet and stared into the box. He reached for his cell at the same time he addressed the manager. "Ma'am, I'm with the Little Rock Police Department. You need to evacuate the building immediately."

The woman's eyes were wide and she remained frozen to the spot.

"Ma'am." Dad shook the woman's arm slightly until she looked at him. "You need to implement your emergency evacuation plan."

The woman nodded.

"Now!" Dad used that *cop tone* of his ... the one Sam didn't like him to use with her.

The woman turned and rushed away.

"Sam, go get Makayla and head to the car." He dialed

as he spoke to her. "Wait for me there." He spoke into the phone. "This is Detective Sanderson, badge number one-one-two-one. I'm at Chenal 9 IMAX Theatre. Request a bomb unit be dispatched to this location immediately."

A bomb?

Sam pulled out her smartphone, opened the camera application, then took a step inside the closet and peered around her father into the box. Metal and wires tangled against what looked like an alarm clock. She held down the shutter button, capturing multiple photographs.

"Samantha! Get Makayla and go to the car." Dad moved her out from the closet and handed her the keys. "Wait for me there. Now." He turned his back on her and spoke into the phone again.

Her pulse thumping, Sam raced to get Makayla.

A bomb? In the theater?

CHAPTER 2

THINGS THAT GO BOOM!

How could Dad do this to her? Making her stay in the parking lot with a uniformed officer while all the action happened inside? It was *so* wrong. She held up her smartphone, videoing the activity as best she could, even though she'd muted the microphone so she could talk freely with her best friend.

"I can't believe this is happening." Makayla's eyes were wide against her smooth, mocha skin.

Turning her attention back to the theater, Sam shook her head. "I know. I can't believe Dad won't let me inside."

"Sam! It's dangerous in there. Didn't you see all the special equipment the bomb squad hauled in there? How can you even think about being inside?"

"That's where the story is. And hey, if it weren't for me, they might not have even found the bomb." Sam continued shooting video in twenty-second segments. "I should at least be able to hear what's going on."

The cop standing beside them grinned at her. "Want me to turn up the radio?"

"Can you? Please?"

He opened the door to his police car and bent inside. Almost immediately, Sam recognized her father's voice booming. "Martin, keep those spectators out. The bomb unit says the device is active."

"Affirmative," cackled back over the radio.

Sam stopped recording and stared at the movie theater. Hearing that the bomb was active made it more real somehow. She suddenly no longer wanted to be inside, no matter that the story took place behind the glass front. But her dad was in there! "Um, how long does it normally take for them to turn the bomb off?" she asked the officer as she turned from the building.

The cop shrugged. "Depends on how complex the bomb is. If they can't defuse it onsite but the device is stable, they'll put it in the bomb-mobile and take it to the shop to take apart."

Who cared about that? Her dad was in there with a live bomb!

Makayla slipped her hand into Sam's. "Your dad will be okay. I've been praying for him and everyone inside."

Even her usual optimism couldn't calm Sam's fears this time.

Sam nodded but returned to staring at the theater. She hadn't realized just how dangerous her dad's job was until now. She couldn't ignore the truth with the threat staring her right in the face.

Her mother's job was always dangerous. As an international journalist, Mom's stories often put her on the front line of danger. Her mom's passion for her career and her telling of the adventures she'd experienced filled Sam with the burning in her chest to have the same type of escapades. She wanted to be the best, just like Mom, and was well aware of the threats associated with the job.

But until today, Sam hadn't considered the daily dangers of Dad's job since he'd been promoted to detective. He wasn't out on the streets, walking up to strange cars that might have a drug-crazed, gun-happy freak behind the wheel. He wasn't chasing down drug dealers or gang members on the city streets down by the riverfront. He shouldn't be in constant danger.

Not like being so close to a live bomb.

"They've defused it!" Dad's voice filled with excitement over the radio.

Sam let out the breath she'd been holding. Now that she'd seen him up close and personal, working in the face of danger, she'd worry about him more. Maybe almost as much as she worried about Mom. But for the moment, he was fine. She was fine. Everyone was fine.

Now she could concentrate on the big story. Who planted the bomb? And why?

What felt like hours later, Dad emerged from the theater and joined her and Makayla in the parking lot. "Let's get you girls home. Y'all look beat."

As if she could sleep now. She and Makayla followed him to his truck and climbed inside.

"Dad, do you have any idea who put the bomb in the theater?"

"Not yet, pumpkin. The bomb unit will go over the device itself and see if there is any forensic evidence." He started the truck, then backed out of the parking space.

"What if they don't find any evidence? Does that mean the person gets away with it?" She pulled out her smartphone and opened the notes application. She punched in comments as fast as her mind raced.

He sighed. "No. It just means it'll take a little longer for the case to get some footing. The bomb unit lieutenant will make a profile based upon the device itself, and that will be the starting point." He met her gaze in his rearview mirror. "Don't go getting any reporting ideas, Sam. This isn't a story for a middle school newspaper. And if you got any photographs of the bomb itself, you need to send them to me and then delete them off your phone."

"Dad, everybody at our school goes to that theater all the time. Of course it's a story for our paper." Was he serious? "And I took the pictures. They're mine."

"Sam, you either send me those pictures and then delete them, or I confiscate your phone. Understand?"

Makayla shoved an elbow in Sam's side.

"Yes, sir." She opened her camera roll on her latest model iPhone and forwarded the pictures. Once they were sent, she deleted them. But she couldn't let the discussion go. She really felt that the bomb was a story for their school paper.

This could give her a scoop right out of the chute. If she was going to be in the running for editor next year, she needed this. "Someone's going to write about it, Dad. At least I was there. I know the truth." Dad wasn't wild about the press ever since a reporter misquoted him months ago and got him in hot water with his boss. "Somebody else might not have all the facts, and no telling what they might print."

"True." Dad flipped on the blinker as he braked for the red light at the intersection of Chenal and Chenal Valley Drive. "But before you run off and start printing articles, let me approve what you submit."

"Dad, that's censorship." She wasn't some little kid, about to spout off without knowing the facts. Yet that's just how he was treating her.

"No, it's smart reporting. We don't want a panic. What if everyone becomes scared and refuses to go back to the theater? The owner could go bankrupt. You don't want to be responsible for something like that, do you?"

"No. But people have the right to know. Don't you think the state newspaper will run an article about the bomb?" Why should she have to get approval for what she witnessed?

"The press will be given information through the proper police channels."

"Then give me that contact." She'd begged her father last year to be put on the press list at the police station, but he'd refused. He'd said that only recognized publications were listed, but she noticed the high school paper seemed to get the information with no problem.

"You know I can't, Sam." Dad whipped the truck into Makayla's driveway.

"Thanks again for taking me, Mr. Sanderson." Makayla opened the truck door and scooted out. "I'll see you at church in the morning."

Sam followed her friend out of the truck, snagged a quick hug, then opened the passenger door and climbed in the front seat.

Dad waited until Makayla was inside the house and turned off the porch light before he backed out. "I know you want to run with the story, and I don't want to hold you back, but there's a proper protocol for reporters on stories such as these."

"You mean where the general public could be in danger?"

He clenched his jaw hard. He was either angry or frustrated. In this case, probably a little of both. "Sam …"

"Dad, this is big for me. I promise I'll be responsible in my reporting. You've got to trust me sometime." It wasn't like she went off half-baked all the time.

"All right." He pulled into the garage, then turned off the engine. "But if you hear a rumor, before you put that in your article, run it by me first, okay?"

"Sure, Dad." She slipped out of the truck and slammed the door. "Thanks for taking us tonight." Without meaning to, he'd given her a head-start on her editor campaign.

She raced into the house. Chewy, her German hunt terrier, met her at the door, jumping and wiggling with excitement. She laughed at her dog's antics as she let the pooch out into the backyard and then bounded up the stairs, not needing to be quiet since Mom was out of town on assignment.

She plopped into the ergonomic chair behind her desk and opened her MacBook Pro, her pride and joy that had been her Christmas present last year. Mom had said if she was serious about being a journalist, then she needed the right equipment. The Mac meant the world to Sam — mainly because it was a statement that her mom believed in her dream. Besides, she had an addiction to gadgets. She just couldn't help herself.

After opening Word, she interlaced her fingers, then stretched them out in front of her, popping her knuckles. She rolled her shoulders before typing in the headline she'd come up with on the way upstairs: Late-Night Show Bombs at Chenal Theater.

Chewy burst into the room, her body wagged by her tail. Dad stuck his head in the door moments later. "Get some sleep. We have church in the morning."

"I will. Just gotta get the emotion down on the page while it's still fresh in my mind."

Dad sighed and tapped the doorframe. "Not too late."

"Only fifteen or so minutes." She looked up from the monitor. "And Dad?"

"Yeah?"

"I'm glad you weren't hurt tonight."

He smiled. "Me, too." He stepped into the room and planted a kiss on her forehead. "No more than fifteen minutes, then bed, okay?"

"Okay."

"Night. Love you."

"Night and love you too, Dad." She focused on the blinking cursor as Dad left.

Chewy jumped up onto her bed and circled twice before she plopped down on the pillows.

Sam typed as she replayed what she'd felt, then put it in article format. When she'd finished, she glanced at the time — five after midnight. Well past the fifteen minutes she'd promised Dad, but this was for her future.

She opened her email, clicked on Aubrey Damas's name, and entered BOMB AT CHENAL 9 in the subject line. Her heart quickened a bit as she typed a quick message telling Aubrey about the bomb and that she'd turn in an article for the first edition of the school's paper. Surely Aubrey wouldn't let her personal feelings against Sam stop her from running the story?

Sam chewed what was once her fingernail and reread her message. It was polite, to the point, and informative. She glanced at Chewy lying on her pillow. "She won't assign the story to someone else, right?"

Chewy stared back with her expressive brown eyes as if to reassure Sam. It didn't work. Sam's gut still tightened as she pressed the button to send the email.

She shut the laptop and dragged herself into the bathroom to brush her teeth. As usual, she turned on the television hidden in the bathroom mirror. She flipped to the national all-news station as she brushed. Nothing of major interest caught her eye, so she turned off the newscast and the bathroom light. As she crawled into bed and turned off the lights, she made up her mind. If Aubrey tried to give the story to someone else, Sam would go straight to Ms. Pape.

Even if that would make Aubrey hate her all the more.

CHAPTER 3

SUNDAY SECRETS

Stop yawning," Makayla whispered, covering her own gaping mouth with her hand.

The youth director, Ms. Martha, kept on talking about the upcoming skate party. Sam shook her head, trying to focus. It was no use. Despite the coolness of the church's youth room with the bright green, blue, and purple paint, Sam's mind wasn't in Sunday school — it was back at home, in her bed. Where her body desperately wanted to be at the moment.

Another yawn pushed out.

"Sam," Makayla hissed.

Suddenly, it was all very funny to Sam. A giggle rose from her chest and escaped. Makayla gawked at her as if she'd sprouted a second head. That made Sam laugh harder.

And louder.

Others turned to stare, which made her giggle even more. Within seconds, it was uncontrollable. Sam held her stomach as she bent. No way would she be able to control the outburst any time soon.

Even Ms. Martha chuckled. "Sounds like someone's giggle box switched on."

Sam shook her head and stood. "I-I. Bath-room." It was all she could get out before she turned and rushed from the room.

She found it hard to catch her breath as she made it down the church's hallway to the ladies' room. Inside, she stared at herself in the mirror, still chuckling. Her face was redder than her shirt.

What was wrong with her? It had to be exhaustion. She hadn't slept well. Visions of her father holding a stick of dynamite had drifted in and out of her dreams all night. That stopped the laughter-fest.

Sam splashed her face with cold water. She dabbed a rough paper towel against her cheeks, which were still pretty red. Her eyes were bloodshot.

She'd been running late this morning, so she hadn't done much with her hair. Normally shiny, thick, and with a hint of a wave, it hung limp today like someone had spilled a bowl of burnt noodles over her head.

Simply put, she looked a mess.

But there was nothing she could do about it now. Sam wadded the paper towel and tossed it into the trash. She reached for the door but froze as she heard voices in the hall.

"Do you think those coalition people were behind the bombing?"

No mistaking that voice: it belonged to Ms. Vanya. Sam's mom had complained more than a few times that Ms. Vanya was one of the biggest gossips around.

"Probably." Ms. Kirkpatrick's nasal voice matched her pinched-looking face. "Those Coalition of Reason heathens? Humph. Did you see those ads they put on the city buses last year? They probably *did* plant the bomb to go off while we were all sitting in the theater today."

Sam knew she should probably stop eavesdropping and go back to her Sunday school room, but the word *bomb* had stopped her in her tracks. Not only because of her article, but also because of her dreams.

"From what I heard," Ms. Vanya continued, "the bomb was set to detonate about thirty minutes into the movie. It had to be some atheists. Who else would want to bomb during such a time?"

"Are you still going?" Ms. Kirkpatrick asked.

"I don't think so. I'm too scared. Are you?"

"Of course. No Satan-lovin' heathens are gonna keep me from walking in victory. That's what they want — for us to not be blessed by watching that movie. That bomb threat has just made me more determined than ever to go. You should, too. Don't be a ninny," said Ms. Kirkpatrick.

Sam held her breath. Her father hadn't even

mentioned the group, but it made perfect sense. The theater had been as sparse as a ghost town last night, and she'd even wondered if it was because *Faithfully HIS* was being shown today in a private viewing to local churches. Had an opposing group done such an act in retaliation?

The door opened right in front of her. Sam gasped and jumped backward.

"Oh, dear, Samantha. You startled me." Ms. Vanya patted her chest. "Are you okay, dear? You look pale."

"You scared me." Her laughing bout was gone for good now.

"Are you sick?" Ms. Kirkpatrick stared through her thick glasses perched low down on her beaked nose.

"N-No, ma'am." Truth be told, the woman scared Sam a bit. Always had. "I best be getting back to my Sunday school class." She inched past the women.

"You have a good day, dear," Ms. Vanya rang out behind her.

"You, too." But Sam didn't stop. She kept a fast walk until she slipped back into the youth group's special room.

Last year, the youth group had come together to redesign their room. They'd painted it white with stripes in green, purple, and blue. The couch cushions matched the green and blue, and the bean bag chairs were purple. Sam's favorite part of the room was the verse scrolled on the wall:

Don't let anyone think less of you because YOU
   ARE young.
Be AN EXAMPLE to all believers in what you teach,
IN THE WAY YOU LIVE, in your love, YOUR
   FAITH, and your purity.

1 Timothy 4:12

"Welcome back, Sam. Things all better now?" Ms. Martha asked.

Heat shot to her cheeks. "Yes, ma'am. Sorry. I don't know what happened to me. I just couldn't stop laughing."

"It happens." Ms. Martha turned her attention back to the entire group and continued her discussion on King David.

"What's wrong with you?" Makayla whispered.

"Up too late. Didn't sleep well." Sam inched closer to her best friend on the couch. "Hey, what do you know about the Coalition of Reason?"

Makayla shot her a strange look. "Why?"

"I'm just wondering if they had anything to do with planting the bomb last night."

"Why would they do that?"

"Girls, is there something you'd like to share?" Ms. Martha crossed her arms over her chest.

The heat returned to Sam's cheeks. "No, ma'am." She ducked her head.

Ms. Martha sighed and sat on the edge of the table in the corner of the front of the room. "We might as well discuss what's on all of yours minds. It's what all the adults are talking about as well."

Everyone gave her their full attention.

"I'm sure most of you heard on the news this morning that a bomb was found in the Chenal theater last night."

The group nodded.

"It's scary to think about, isn't it? Especially when many of you plan to go to the special viewing of *Faithfully HIS* today with your family," said Ms. Martha.

"Are they still planning to show the movie?" Ava Kate asked.

"My mom said there's no way we're going." Lissi shifted in her seat. Her skin was a shade darker than Makayla's smooth mocha complexion, but Lissi's smile could brighten the darkest of rooms. Sam liked that about her. "Mom said that the bomb was definitely put there by someone who hates Christians. She said if they tried to bomb it and that failed, there's no telling what they'll do next."

Sam gnawed on her cuticle. She hadn't considered that possibility. While she and Dad hadn't planned on attending the movie, many of her friends were going with their families, like Makayla and her mom, dad, and little sister.

"As of this morning, I hadn't heard whether the theater owner had decided to still show the movie or not." Ms. Martha stretched her legs out in front of her, crossing them at the ankles. "But let's talk about how we feel about the bomb. It's scary, isn't it?"

"My mom's really freaked out over it," Jeremy said. "Dad told her to stop being hysterical or he was going to turn off the news."

Everyone chuckled nervously, but Sam understood. It *was* scary. She remembered how scared she was for her father last night. Just thinking about it now made her heartbeat kick up a notch.

"We were there."

Everyone stared at Makayla.

"Me and Sam. With her dad. They're the ones who found the bomb."

The room erupted with questions and comments.

"Oh, wow."

"What'd it look like?"

"How freaky is that!"

"What did you do?"

"Where was it?"

Ms. Martha held up her hands. "Shh, everybody. You can't all talk at once." She gave Sam and Makayla a smile. "Girls, why don't you tell everyone what happened?"

"Well, we went out to get a drink, but we saw a light shining through the crack of the supply closet door in the bathroom, then Makayla spilled her drink all over my dad's pants and the manager came and I told her about the light in the supply room and we had to go there to get a mop anyway . . ." Sam sucked in air.

"What?"

"I don't get it."

"Huh?"

Again, Ms. Martha held up her hand. "Shh."

Makayla shook her head and explained what had happened. While she gave the long version, Sam mentally made a list of things she needed to research for her article, like the coalition. She needed to see if there were any news reports of groups protesting the *Faithfully HIS* showing.

Would Dad tell her if the theater had received any threats?

"I know it's very scary, as are so many of the events in this day and age. Terrorism. Violence. But this has hit very close to home." Ms. Martha had everyone's attention again. "I'll admit I get scared when I hear of such violent events on the news. But can anyone tell me what Scripture says about fear?"

The room grew quiet.

Ms. Martha laughed. "This isn't a quiz."

Lissi cleared her throat. "The Bible tells us not to be afraid."

"Right. What else?" Ms. Martha asked.

"But," Sandy said, pushing her glasses back up the bridge of her nose, "doesn't the Bible tell us over and over again to fear God. If fear doesn't come from God, why does He want us to fear Him?"

"Yeah, I don't get that either," Daniel looked to Ms. Martha. He might be in high school, but he never looked down on the younger kids in the youth group. Sam liked that about him. That and his amazing smile and only one dimple. On the right side. Not that she'd really noticed.

"I don't have all the black-and-white answers, guys. What I do know is that the fear of the Lord that's talked about in Scripture is a reverent fear and awe, not a scared-of-the-boogeyman type of fear. Does that make sense?"

"Kinda," Sandy answered. "But I still don't understand why so many bad things happen to Christian people."

"That, my sweet, is an answer I don't have." Ms. Martha smiled as the tower bells chimed. "And the discussion of that will have to wait until another week." She held out her hands to the group. "Let's pray."

After Ms. Martha dismissed the group, Sam nudged Makayla. "Are y'all still going to the movie this afternoon?"

She shrugged as she led the way into the sanctuary. "Mom doesn't want to, but Dad says we shouldn't be bullied by acts of violence."

Basically the same thing Ms. Kirkpatrick had said. "What do *you* think?" Sam asked. She didn't want her best friend in danger.

"On one hand, I want to see the movie. On the other, I'm scared. But after hearing Ms. Martha, I wonder if I should just trust God to protect us."

Sam's mouth went spitless. It was one thing to say that, but to put their lives on the line for trust … sometimes Makayla's optimistic outlook defied Sam's reality.

"After all, He protected us last night. And your dad. Right?" Makayla asked.

She had a point.

"So I guess whatever the 'rents decide will be okay with me." Makayla stopped at a pew and stared at Sam. "Why? Do you want to go to the movie with us? I'm sure Mom and Dad would love to have you come along."

"That's not an option any longer, girls." Dad stepped into the pew behind Sam.

"What?" Sam asked. He wouldn't let her go? She hadn't exactly thought about whether she really wanted to go or not, but for Dad just to say no period? That wasn't fair.

"The theater isn't showing any movie today." Dad sat down and tugged on Sam's shirt.

She plopped down beside him. "Why not?"

Makayla chased after her little sister, Chloe, pulling her into the pew in front of Sam's.

"It's a crime scene, pumpkin. We aren't finished gathering all the evidence there."

Something about his tone ...

"*We*, Dad?"

He nodded as he pulled out the bulletin and pretended to be very interested in the sermon notes. "Um, yeah. My captain called me this morning and gave me the case. I'll be working with the bomb unit."

Dad would be the one with all the information on the case? This was too easy.

Hello, editor of the school newspaper ... here I come.

CHAPTER 4

BLOGGING ABOUT

I have to tell you all something exciting," said Ms. Pape, the eighth grade English teacher and sponsor of the school newspaper. She stood in front of the newspaper staff, wearing a wide smile.

Stuffiness filled the room. The last heat wave of summer caused the school to run the air-conditioner on high, but it still never got really cool in the old building's wings.

"The school administration has approved our request for a school blog."

Everyone began murmuring. Sam turned to Celeste, sitting beside her. "Did you know about this?"

Celeste, a fellow seventh grader who was also on the cheer squad with Sam, shook her head. "Must've been something they asked about last year." Sixth graders weren't allowed to be on newspaper staff.

"Aubrey has made decisions on which topic each reporter will blog about." Ms. Pape smiled again. "We've made a list of topics that will need to be addressed, and Aubrey will let you know which assignment you receive each week. Careful consideration has been given to each topic, as well as which staff member to assign to it. Aubrey will be adjusting and rotating so everyone will have an opportunity to post at least once a week."

Every one of them? Sam elbowed Celeste. "At least she can't keep us from writing," she whispered. Aubrey had made no secret that she resented Sam being on the newspaper staff. She knew Sam wanted to be editor-in-chief. Plus Aubrey just thought all of the seventh graders were *beneath* the eighth graders.

Ms. Pape moved to her desk in the front corner of the room. "When there's breaking news, Aubrey will assign reporters to cover these topics."

Aubrey began by informing the group of the four daily topics: main headlines, sports, student corner, and teacher tips. She assigned four reporters to each topic. Sam swallowed her groan when her name was assigned — teacher tips. Nobody wanted to talk to teachers about tips to get better grades, improve study habits, and boring stuff like that. Surely no one wanted to read it. Leave it to Aubrey to put her in the worst category.

Finally, all the staffers were assigned their topics, then Aubrey stood in front of the classroom-turned-newspaper room. "Now, about the Chenal theater bombing assignment," she said.

Sam inched to the edge of her seat. Her feet moved under her chair, her toes pressed onto the dirty floor. Her knees bounced up and down.

All day long, everyone had been talking about the bomb and the cancellation of the movie viewing. Sam had bit her tongue over and over, refusing to give any information. She wanted to wait until now, last period and in the newsroom, to let everyone know she was *in the know*.

Aubrey hugged her clipboard. "We have a good start with the article *Samantha* turned in as an eyewitness account, which I'll load up on the blog in a moment." Of course, she called Sam by her full name just to irritate her. Aubrey glanced over the room. "But I think we need a more seasoned reporter to continue the assignment on our blog as updates become available through the police." She blushed a little and smiled at Kevin Haynes, the blond haired eighth grader sitting in the front row.

Everybody knew Aubrey had a crush on the blue-eyed quarterback — what girl in school didn't? Kevin was the most popular guy at the middle school, and in addition to being the star of the football team, he was also president of the student council, captain of the debate team, and leader of the Alpha gifted program.

Word in the newsroom from the eighth graders was

that Aubrey always gave Kevin the best assignments, even though he wasn't the best reporter. Everybody knew Kevin cared about football more than anything else.

But this bomb story was too important to take a backseat to sports.

Sam couldn't stand it. She jumped up, nearly knocking over her chair. "I want the assignment," she said.

All the eighth graders seated in the front row, including Kevin, turned to stare at her. Some of the girls even smirked, especially Nikki Cole, Aubrey's best friend. Their expressions were all the same: How dare a seventh grader have the nerve to request such a cool assignment?

Heat flooded her face, and Sam was pretty certain it was redder than Aubrey's at the moment, but she couldn't let this one go. She had to stand up for herself. For the story. She swallowed, then took in a deep breath. "I mean, my dad's overseeing the case, so I'll get all the information first." That wasn't *exactly* the way it was, but . . .

"Your dad is heading up the investigation?" Aubrey asked, frowning at her.

Sam nodded. "He'll be working with the bomb unit."

Murmurs sounded around the room.

She ignored the whispers and cleared her throat. "Closely. He'll know all the facts of the case." Not that he'd share them with her, but he might. If he realized how important this story was to her making editor of the *Senator Speak* next year. Surely he'd understand how this could make or break her start in journalism.

Ms. Pape smiled at Sam from behind her desk. "That's a great connection, Aubrey. Maybe it's possible we can even scoop the high school paper. We'd certainly get more exposure for the blog."

If the middle school broke a big story before the high school, the editor got some serious respect on the high school campus. It rarely happened, so Aubrey hesitated. Sam raked her top teeth over her bottom lip. Aubrey was probably weighing the choices — make Kevin really happy with her and maybe have him invite her to the back-to-school social, or get a head start on her high school reputation.

Sam had no doubt which way she'd go if the decision were hers. She'd wanted to be a journalist ever since she could remember. Mom's stories were amazing. Her travels ... her experiences ... Sam wanted all that for herself one day.

But the decision wasn't Sam's, or even Ms. Pape's. It was Aubrey's. Even though it was clear Ms. Pape thought Sam should get the assignment, the teacher who acted as the newspaper's sponsor would let Aubrey make the decision, right or wrong. She lectured many times that this was how news people learned: by making the hard choices and living with the consequences.

"Well, since her dad's on the case and all ..." Aubrey's blush came back as she shot Kevin a sly look, then looked over the room, but avoided eye-contact with Sam. "I'll give Samantha the assignment." Now she did stare right at Sam. "I'll expect you to submit your blog pieces early morning before school until the case is solved. Keep your articles new and fresh. If you don't, I'll give the assignment to someone else. Understood?"

Sam nodded, not trusting herself to speak. She'd just been handed a once-in-a-lifetime chance to shine. She wouldn't mess it up.

Aubrey made a note on her clipboard, then looked over the group. "Good. Now, moving on, we need to talk about the back-to-school dance being held next month. Who wants to cover the preparations?"

The editor's words faded out. Sam slowly exhaled and plopped back into her chair. She couldn't really believe she'd actually gotten the assignment! She swallowed the victory yell rising from her gut. She couldn't wait to tell Makayla. She'd have to hurry to see Makayla at the lockers to at least tell her the news. They wouldn't be able to talk about it until later because she had cheer practice this afternoon and Mac had karate.

Lana Wilson, one of the other seventh grade reporters, tapped her from behind.

Sam glanced over her shoulder.

Grinning, Lana gave her a thumbs-up. Lana had transferred from another school at the end of last year and had gotten assigned to the newspaper staff, a fact Aubrey wasn't too happy about. Aubrey and Lana had a mutual dislike of one another, and neither tried too hard to hide the fact.

Sam smiled back, then faced front. She couldn't pay attention to Aubrey, but she could look like she was listening. All she could think about was the next article. The first one, more of an eyewitness account, Aubrey seemed to like, but Sam needed to take a different angle with the next one. She needed to show her diversity as a reporter, get a different tone for the blog.

If only Mom were home. No, on second thought, Sam wanted to do this all on her own. *Needed* to. If she wanted her parents to take her goals to become a journalist seriously, she had to make progress on her own. Mom always said that a successful reporter stood on their own and ferretted out the truth for the truth's sake. Whatever *that* meant.

The bell rang, and Sam sprinted to her locker.

Makayla was already there. "Why are you rushing?" she asked.

"Guess what?" Sam grinned so big it hurt her cheeks.

Makayla shut her locker. "What? Hurry up, I've got to get on the bus before the eighth graders. They take up whole seats with just one person, and I don't want to have to sit in the front row with the sixth graders." She slung her backpack over her shoulder.

"I got the bomb articles!"

"Aubrey gave you the assignment?" Makayla's eyes went wide.

Sam nodded. "The paper's starting a blog, and my posts have to be fresh, but I got it."

Makayla hugged her. "Congratulations! I'll be home from karate practice by five. Call then and you can tell me all the details and explain about the blog."

"Thanks." Sam opened her locker. "Now get to your bus so you don't have to sit with the sixth graders."

Grinning, Makayla gave her another quick hug, then dashed toward the row of buses lined up in front of the school.

Sam grabbed her own backpack and her duffle with her cheer practice outfit, slammed her locker shut, and headed down the ramp to the girls' locker room to change.

The locker room was more than just stuffy, it was hot. The school's automatic timer on the air-conditioning unit turned off at two in an effort to conserve electricity. Those who had to use the locker room after school nearly died of heat exhaustion before they even made it to practice. *Gross.*

A couple of other cheerleaders waved at Sam as they left. Several of the girls' basketball members huddled in groups, talking and giggling.

Sam could barely concentrate. Already, her mind kept going over the next article she'd write. She changed in record time, stowed her stuff in her cubby, then headed down the empty hall to the gym. She slowed as she heard voices coming from one of the offices the various coaches used.

"Did you hear about Bobby Milner's radio interview this morning?" asked Mrs. Holt, the cheerleading coach.

"No. What'd he say now?" Ms. Christian, the girls' basketball coach, answered.

"I didn't get to hear it myself, but my husband did. Apparently Milner said he was glad no one got hurt with the bomb incident, but that it should make the theater owner think twice about showing such religious movies." Mrs. Holt's voice sounded like she'd just gotten a whiff of the stench from the boys' locker room.

Sam held her breath, stopping outside the office door and pressing against the cinderblock wall. What radio station had this been on?

"You've got to be kidding me! What, is he just begging the police to name him as the prime suspect or what?" Ms. Christian's tone was even worse.

"Shouldn't surprise anyone," Mrs. Holt said. "Not with the way he's always spouting off his atheist ideas to anybody who'll listen."

Ms. Christian laughed. "He is a bit of a menace to society, but do you think he's capable of planting a bomb?"

Sam crossed her arms over the *Cheer! Cheer! Cheer!* shirt she wore. She was clearly eavesdropping, which Dad warned her all the time not to do, but this was also research for her articles to help her future career. Mom would understand.

"Maybe. He's really gotten into some hot spots in his quest lately." Mrs. Holt said.

"I think he's looking more for public attention than actually doing anything harmful. Then again, who can tell with people like that?" said Ms. Christian.

"Isn't that the truth? It seems nobody *really* knows anybody these days." Mrs. Holt sighed loudly. "I'd better get out to the squad."

Sam moved down the hall, careful to keep her head ducked as she hurried.

"I need to check on the team. Did you hear we're projected to go to regionals this year?" Ms. Christian's voice grew fainter.

"I did. That's really good," Mrs. Holt answered.

"I hope we can — "

Sam pushed into the gym, her mind racing faster than the football team members sprinting on the practice field. It wasn't like she intended to eavesdrop, but now that she'd heard about this Bobby Milner, she needed to find out what she could about him. It was her duty as a journalist.

She couldn't wait to get home and do some research on the internet. She could just ask Dad who Bobby Milner was, but she'd rather look him up on the internet. Then when she asked Dad, officially for the paper, it'd show him she was serious and had done her homework.

Impress him with her insight.

CHAPTER 5

A REPORTER'S GUT INSTINCT

Listen to this, straight from what the radio station posted on their site. This is what they say about him." Sam adjusted her Bluetooth earpiece and read off the internet as she moved through the motions of the cheer they'd learned in practice. " 'Bobby Milner is an active member of the Arkansas Society of Freethinkers, an organization of secular individuals whose goals are to build a supportive and active community, promote public acceptance of nonbelievers, and defend science education and the separation of church and state.' "

What exactly did that mean?

She stared at the picture of Mr. Milner the radio station had posted. He was younger than Sam had thought, only about thirty or so. For some reason, after listening to him, she'd thought he would be like fifty or something.

Makayla made clicking noises with her tongue over the phone line. "Hey, isn't that the group who protested the picture of the Ten Commandments in that judge's private chambers in the city courthouse? They were on the news and everything, right?"

"I think so." Chewy jumped up on the bed, her entire body wagging. Sam smiled and reached over to scratch behind her ears. "The transcript of Bobby Milner's interview reads just like Mrs. Holt said her husband heard. He said, 'I'm relieved no one got hurt with the bomb incident, but it should make Frank Hughes think twice about allowing the showing of such religious movies. Atheists can feel isolated when the religious community is so organized and outspoken on issues. This is but one of many examples.' "

Goodness, what would Ms. Martha and Pastor Patterson make of Mr. Milner's comments? Hmm. Maybe she could get a statement from Pastor for her next article. She'd need someone to go on record about Mr. Milner being a suspect. *If* he was a suspect. Surely he was — with the radio interview, how could he not be? Maybe Dad would give her a quote.

"I'm assuming Frank Hughes is the theater owner?" Makayla asked, interrupting Sam's thoughts.

"Yep." Sam glanced at the digital frame hanging on the wall beside her desk. Instead of photos, there were matted articles written by her mom that had been scanned in and flashed as a slide-show. Articles where things weren't always what they seemed and Mom had helped uncover the truth. Maybe this story was Sam's chance to do the same thing.

Clicking sounded over the line. "Let me do some checking and see if I can find anything on him." Some checking? Sam could hold her own on a computer, but Makayla was a ninja-genius on the computer. There wasn't much she couldn't find out using a computer. "Thanks, Mac."

Sophia's and Makayla's addiction to technology had landed them both in EAST this year. The Environmental And Spatial Technology class allowed them access to some of the newest software and hardware on the market. Their EAST classes focused on student-driven service projects by using teamwork and cutting-edge technology. The EAST classroom had the coolest computers, laptops, software, and accessories, including GPS/GIS mapping tools, architectural and CAD design software, 3D animation suites, virtual reality development, and more. The kids in EAST could identify problems in the community and then use these tools to develop solutions, usually working with other groups.

More typing sounded over Sam's headset as Makayla said, "No worries. Hey, did you hear Nikki's party next weekend has been cancelled?"

"No." Why would she? She hadn't been invited.

"Yeah. Heard her parents are separating," said Makayla.

"Oh. That's harsh." Even though Nikki and Aubrey were best friends, which meant Nikki shunned her, Sam felt bad for her. Nobody should have to deal with something like that.

"Yeah, we should pray for her family," Makayla said.

A car door slammed outside, triggering Chewy's enthusiastic barking. Sam moved to the window and peered past the blackout curtains. Dad stepped out of the unmarked police car, his hair looking like he'd shoved his hands through it a lot. Mom said that was a sign he'd been doing a lot of thinking. "Dad's home, so I gotta go. I'll be praying for Nikki and her parents. Email or text if you find out anything interesting on Bobby Milner."

The front door slammed. "Sam?" Dad called out as his keys clattered into the wooden bowl on the entry table.

"Coming," Sam yelled, then said, "Gotta go, Mac."

She tossed her earpiece onto the desk and hurried to meet her dad. She found him in the kitchen, checking the roast he'd put in the crock pot before they'd left this morning. He'd already secured his gun and badge in his bedroom lockbox.

Sam's stomach rumbled as the yummy smell hit her. "Hi, Daddy. How was your day?" She reached for the can of green beans sitting on the counter.

"Long." He kissed the top of her head. "Why don't you start the water to boil for the mashed potatoes while I change?" Without waiting for an answer, he headed down the hall to his and Mom's bedroom.

Sam mentally rehearsed her questions as she put the green beans in the pot on the stove and started the water boiling for the potatoes. Mom always made homemade mashed potatoes, but her and Dad? Well, they used the instant ones. If there was enough salt and butter on them, she could barely tell the difference. Not that she'd let Mom know.

When Dad came back, Sam dumped the salad mix into bowls and set the table. The potatoes were done in a few minutes and they sat across the table, smelling the delicious food. Dad said grace and then started in on the usual conversation. "How was school today?"

"You won't believe what we got." Without waiting for a response, Sam filled him in on the school news blog. "Isn't that awesome?"

"That's very nice," Dad said, but he seemed distracted. And tired.

"Anything new on the case?" she asked.

"We're waiting for the bomb unit to finish its forensic investigation."

What did that mean? "What about the theater? Is it open again?"

Dad nodded and finished chewing. "We finished processing this morning, so Mr. Hughes opened this afternoon with a couple of discounted showings." He shook his head as he reached for his glass of milk.

"Didn't look like much of a crowd, though, when I passed by on my way home."

"Is that bad?" she asked.

"Well, I imagine matinees are slower since you kids are back in school, but the place looked emptier than I've ever seen."

"Because people are scared of another bomb?"

"Probably." Dad swallowed. "Sam, you know you can't share any of this, right?"

"Dad, I got the assignment! I'm the reporter assigned to the bomb case." And she needed something for her article. Something juicy, or her career would be over before it even started. "Dad, I need something *official* for my blog post tomorrow."

"I wish you'd let this one go, pumpkin."

"Dad! This could kick off my career."

"I see." He let out a sigh and swiped a napkin across his mouth. He smoothed it before setting it back in his lap. "After you finish the dishes, I'll let you ask a few questions, just enough to get something for your article tomorrow. Okay?"

She grinned. "Deal."

He smiled back. "How was cheerleading practice? When's the first game?"

The rest of dinner lagged. She answered Dad's questions and offered input, trying to be patient. She didn't want to irritate him by asking questions too early, since he said he would answer them after dinner. Soon enough, though, they were finished and she cleared the table.

Excitement pushed her to put away the leftovers, load the dishwasher, scrub out the crock pot, and wipe down the counters in record time. Her mind kept flipping through the questions she wanted to ask, but she knew Dad wouldn't talk until everything was spic and span. *Had the bomb squad found out anything yet?* Maybe there were fingerprints on the actual bomb. That'd be cool.

Or maybe they had another lead. What if somebody had used a similar bomb to actually blow something up? That'd be a pattern, right?

Finally done with chores, she grabbed her iPhone and opened the recorder application, sat down on the couch in the living room, and stared at Dad sitting in his recliner with his feet up.

He let out a sigh and lowered the newspaper he'd been reading. "Go ahead and ask. I can tell you're about to burst."

She let out a slow breath. Calm. Professional. She pressed the record button on the app. "Has any person or group taken credit for the bomb?"

Dad's eyebrows shot up. "Well, I wasn't expecting that."

"What? For someone to claim the bomb as theirs?" she asked.

"No, for you to ask the question." He gave a small smile. "Well done, Ms. Sanderson."

Heat pushed up her neck. "Thanks."

The smile slid off his face as he sat up straighter in his recliner. "To answer your question, no. No one person or any group has contacted us to accept responsibility for the bomb."

"What kind of bomb was it?"

"The bomb unit is still analyzing the actual device," Dad said.

She glanced at her smartphone to make sure it was recording properly. "Why the theater?"

"We don't have any solid leads on why the bomb was left at that particular location at that particular time."

Sam remembered what she'd heard Ms. Vanya tell Ms. Kirkpatrick at church yesterday. "Is it true that the bomb was set to go off when the local churches would be having their private showing of *Faithfully HIS*?" she asked.

Dad frowned. "Where did you hear that?"

She shrugged. A reporter never revealed her sources, even if they didn't know they were sources. "Is it true?"

"Sam, I need to know where you heard that. The exact time of detonation hasn't been released to the general public yet."

"I can't tell you, Dad. You know I can't tell you who my sources are." Especially when she'd gotten the information by eavesdropping, something Dad was always warning her not to do. But now she wondered: How did Ms. Vanya know?

He rubbed his chin. "Well, I suppose it's okay to confirm since it'll be in tomorrow's press conference. Yes, the bomb's timer was set to detonate thirty minutes after the posted start time of the movie."

"When will the press conference be tomorrow?"

"When you're in school." Dad still wore the frown.

"Could I skip — "

"No. Don't even ask. You won't miss school to attend a press conference."

She knew that *bulldog* look — eyebrows drawn down, lips puckered tight: he wasn't going to budge on this one. "Will there be a written statement? Something you could bring home to me?"

"Yes. I'll bring home the statement that's released to the press." He sighed. "Now, go finish up your homework."

"Just one more question." She caught the sag of his eyes. "Please. Just one more."

"Okay."

"Do the police consider Bobby Milner a suspect in this attempted bombing?" she asked.

Dad stiffened his spine and kicked down the footrest of his recliner. "What? Why would he be a suspect?"

What a response! Sam tingled all over. Mom always said body language answered most questions. "Well, he belongs to the Arkansas Society of Freethinkers and has been pretty outspoken against religion. And he was on the radio today, spouting off about Christians alienating non-believers."

"It's not a crime to go on the radio and state your beliefs."

"But I read the transcript, Daddy. And listened to recorded portions up on YouTube. It sounds like if he wasn't involved, he fully supported the bomb being there."

"You can't make assumptions, Sam. You can't accuse someone of a crime without proof." He wore the bull-dog look again.

"Isn't that what being a suspect is all about? Proof's not been found but is being looked for?" she asked.

The little muscles in his jaw jumped. "You want an official statement about suspects?"

Her heart raced as her mouth went dry. She nodded.

"We have no comment on any suspects at this time." He lifted the newspaper, blocking his face from her view. "This interview is over. Go finish your homework."

Sam stopped recording and went to her room, her heart pounding. She called the theater to speak with Mr. Hughes for a possible comment, but all she got was the automatic recording. She checked her email. One from Makayla that read:

Robert "Bobby" Milner was arrested for domestic abuse last December, but his wife dropped the charges. Couldn't

find anything else interesting. See you in the morning.

So Mr. Milner had a record of violence? Interesting.

Sam quickly wrote her article while the ideas were still fresh in her mind. As she neared the end of her piece, she stood and paced. Had Dad really used the *no comment* thing on her? Seriously? Such a lame avoidance technique.

She must be onto something.

Her cell rang, making her jump. She reached for the phone, then smiled wide as she recognized the number on the caller-ID. "Hi, Mom." She crossed her legs, rocking on her bed to get comfortable for a good talk.

"Hey there, my girl. How are you?" Mom always sounded like the person she talked to was the only thing she was interested in.

"Great," Sam said, then launched into telling her mom all about the bomb and the blog and getting the assignment.

Mom laughed when Sam paused to take a breath. "Wow, honey, that's awesome."

Sam leaned back against the pillows propped against the headboard. "Thanks, Mom." Heat spread from her stomach to her toes. Praise from Mom was like ... well, it was like the best.

"I'm sure you're a little worried about Dad, aren't you?" Mom asked.

Even miles away, Mom *got* it. "Yeah. A little," Sam answered.

"I understand."

"You do?" Sam asked.

"I do. And I worry about you, too."

Sam smiled.

"Do you know what makes me feel better about both of you, when I'm away?" Mom asked.

"What?"

"Every morning, I pray for God to hold you both in His hands. And I mentally picture myself putting you and your dad in God's hands. It's a powerful image, and it makes me not worry so much because I know there's no better place for you to be."

Wow. Sam closed her eyes and thought of the same image. It *was* powerful. "Thanks, Mom."

"You're welcome, sweetie." A rustling sounded in the background. "Listen, I have to get back to work. I just wanted to talk to you before you went to bed. I love you."

"G'night, Mom. I love you, too."

Sam stared at her article, then stood and paced again. She needed to make it good ... strong.

Something Mom would be proud of her for writing.

CHAPTER 6

THE TROUBLE WITH RESEARCH

… but it's a fact the bomb was set to detonate approximately 30 minutes into the movie showing. Police offer the standard "no comment" when asked about suspects, but no one should ignore the fact that Bobby Milner, member of a local "freethinking" group, went on our local radio station and said, "This should make Frank Hughes think twice about allowing the showing of such religious movies."

Frank Hughes is the owner of the theater. He was unavailable for comment.

Robert "Bobby" Milner was arrested last December for a violent offense.

What do YOU think? Should Bobby Milner be considered a suspect in the attempted bombing? Sound Off,

Senators. Leave a comment with your thoughts. ~ Sam Sanderson, reporting.

"Your blog post this morning has gotten over a hundred comments already," Ms. Pape told Sam as soon as she entered the newsroom for last period on Tuesday afternoon.

Sam stared at her. "Really? Is that good?" She dumped her books onto the desk.

"It's a great response," Ms. Pape said as Aubrey joined her. "Especially for the first day the blog's been live." She didn't smile. "Some of the comments are referring to Mr. Milner's arrest record. I'm still not sure I should have allowed you to include it in the piece."

"It's a matter of public record, Ms. Pape. Just like Aubrey agreed this morning," Sam said. She was still impressed that the editor had put the news before her personal dislike of Sam.

Aubrey faced the teacher, turning her back on Sam. "May I speak with you for a moment, Ms. Pape?" She cut her eyes over her shoulder at Sam. "At your desk?"

As soon as they moved to Ms. Pape's desk, Celeste and Lana surrounded Sam. Lana slid on top of the desk. "You are rockin' it, girl. Good going."

"Did the other posts get comments, too?" Sam gnawed at the corner of her nail.

Celeste grinned. "Sports got four, student corner got two, and teacher tips got one. Yours has one hundred and four, as of last hour." Her smile spread even wider, the freckles across the bridge of her nose seeming to dance.

Sam resisted the urge to jump into a toe-touch right there in the classroom. With a student body of about eight hundred, having over a hundred comments seemed pretty good to her.

"And the comments are great. They aren't just lame posts. People are talking about Mr. Milner and the bomb. I spent all last period in computer lab, and Mrs. Forge let us check out the blog." Lana swung her legs back and forth, her jewel-studded boots rubbing against the leg of the desk with every pass, making a *scritch-scratch* noise.

Sam's throat got a little tight. Dad had told her not to accuse someone without proof.

Scritch-scratch ... scritch-scratch.

But she wasn't really accusing Mr. Milner of anything. She just wrote what was already up on the radio station's website.

Scritch-scratch ... scritch-scratch.

That wasn't really accusing him, right?

"Good work, Sam." The voice behind her made her mouth go dry.

She turned, forcing her smile to hold in place. "T-Thanks, Luke." Heat filled her cheeks and she dropped her gaze to the floor.

Ohmygummybears! Ohmygummybears!

Luke Jensen, the cutest boy in seventh grade. Well, at least to Sam. He had sandy blond, wavy hair and eyes that reminded her of dark chocolate. They'd gone to school together since kindergarten, but lately, every time she got near him, Sam's mind refused to remember how to speak. As if the English language wasn't her native tongue.

"You're a good reporter," he said.

Her head shot up. His face was a little red, too. She didn't even bother answering, just smiled.

Luke flashed a dimpled grin, then headed off to join the other guys who circled in the back corner and talked sports.

Sam sat with her tongue still tied into a knot as Aubrey stalked to the front of the room. "Okay, people, listen up."

Lana slipped off the desk and into a chair beside Celeste and Sam. Everybody took a seat and focused on the editor-in-chief.

"While Ms. Pape and I go through the comments and respond as we see fit, those of you who have blog posts due in the morning can do research in the media center. For those of you who don't, we still have the bi-monthly paper to put out, so you can help Kevin and Nikki with the layouts," Aubrey said.

What, nothing else? Sam felt more than a little disappointed that Aubrey didn't even bother to mention her post. Everybody in school was talking about her blog post. Ms. Pape had seemed impressed with the number of comments, even if she had been a bit nervous. No wonder — Sam had had to argue with her about leaving in the part about Mr. Milner's past record. They'd gone round and round before school this morning until finally, and surprisingly, Aubrey had pointed out that an arrest record was a matter of public record, and as long as Sam didn't stray from the facts of the record readily available to the public, it could be included. Ms. Pape had reluctantly agreed.

"Come on, let's go to the media center." Celeste grabbed Sam's arm. "I have the student corner tomorrow and need to find some stuff on Charlie Lacey. Do you know him?" She waited while Sam scooped up her books before she led the way out of the newsroom and down the breezeway toward the media center.

"Doesn't he play basketball or something? He's in eighth grade, I think." Sam's mind was already on her next blog post. At least Makayla had study hall this period, so she would be in the media center. She could help.

Sam and Celeste quietly entered the oversized room. No way did they want to make noise and bring the wrath of Mrs. Forge. She had short gray hair that stuck out all over her head and glasses that made her eyes look bigger than a frog's.

Celeste headed to the corner where some of her friends sat around one of the round tables. Sam scanned the tables for Makayla, and finally she spied her in the back corner, her eyes glued to a monitor. Sam made her way over and eased into the seat beside Makayla.

"What are you doing in here?" Makayla whispered.

"Working on my next story. What about you?" Sam nodded toward the computer. "Going boldly where no one has gone before?"

Makayla wrinkled her nose and snorted. "Ha ha. I'm finishing my homework. I want to have it done before I get home. Mom was in homework master-mode last night. Standing over my shoulder, checking every little thing, even though I told her I knew I'd done it all right."

"What's up with that?" Sam asked. "Everyone knows you're brilliant."

Makayla shrugged. "Some homeschooling friend of hers said at karate practice the other night that kids in public schools score lower on tests or something. I hope she's not gonna be like this all year. I'll go crazy."

"Crazier than you already are, you mean?" Sam laughed as Makayla nudged her. "You always get the highest score of anybody in our grade. Your mom's just being weird."

"Tell me about it." Makayla opened the internet. "So, what do you want to put in your next article?"

"Gotta be something different." Aubrey had been very clear that everything had to be fresh and new and informative, or she'd hand the assignment off to someone else. She would be looking for a reason to snatch it away from Sam and give it to Kevin or someone. Sam didn't want that to happen.

"What if you ask your dad to take you to the theater tonight? Maybe you could talk to the owner," said Makayla. "Or maybe you could talk to someone in the bomb unit. Your dad could tell you who."

"Maybe." That was a good idea, but she didn't think Dad would be willing to help her in her reporting. To tell the truth, Sam wanted to do it on her own, to prove to her dad that she was mature enough to be taken seriously.

Makayla lifted a pen and began to doodle on the notebook beside the keyboard. Nothing new there — if she was idle, she was drawing. Sam smiled at the anime faces, all with hair covering one eye; the sunflower; the unicorn; the bus; the ...

Wait a minute. Bus. Why was that sticking in Sam's mind? "Bus," she whispered.

"What?" Makayla whispered back.

"Hang on, let me think." Sam closed her eyes. Bus. Buses. Ms. Kirkpatrick's nasal voice ...

Her eyes shot open. "Search 'bus ads in Little Rock' in Google," said Sam.

Makayla gave her a funny look, but typed it into the search engine. Within seconds, the results loaded. Sam leaned over and scanned the results.

Sam clicked on one of the links and skimmed the information until she found what she needed. "Listen," she whispered. " 'The Central Arkansas Coalition of Reason purchased over five thousand dollars' worth of anti-God ads to run on the Central Arkansas Transit Authority buses serving Little Rock. The ads read: *Are you good without God? Millions are.'* "

Makayla shook her head. "Oh yeah, I remember now. Mom got upset about those ads."

"Why?" Sam asked.

"A judge ruled the ads fell under the free speech law. Mom said the liberals were going to ruin our democracy altogether."

Sam didn't respond. Her mom often talked about free speech and how every journalist should fully support the law. Mom said that even though this coalition pushed the wrong message, they should have the right to take out an ad stating their ideas. But Sam didn't want to argue the point right now with her best friend, so she clicked the mouse to scroll down the page. "The local spokesperson is Jessica Townsend."

"Never heard of her." Makayla leaned closer to the monitor. "What does it say about her?"

"She 'wants to bring together humanistic, secular, and nontheistic organizations in the Little Rock area in a nonviolent manner,' " Sam read.

"Is that why her group went to federal court to get those stupid ads put on the buses? They ran them the two weeks of all the big revivals in town," said Makayla.

"How do you remember that?" Sam asked.

"Because a friend of Mom's was the planner of one of the revivals. Mom got pretty upset about it all. Don't you remember it being on the news and all?"

"Yeah. Now I do." Sam nodded. "The *About Us* part of their site says they proclaim 'the understanding of what is good relies on human reason and compassion, and not on theistic or supernatural beliefs.' "

"So they're basically saying that everything good is from humans being reasonable and compassionate?" Makayla rolled her eyes. "They think God has nothing to do with it?"

"That's how I understand it." Sam had reviewed almost a year's worth of the high school paper's format and how they managed to link one story to another, so she had several ideas for articles. Linking the coalition to the bombing would be an amazing hook.

"These people are crazy enough to plant a bomb," said Makayla.

"Maybe not," Sam answered.

Makayla narrowed her eyes and shifted to stare Sam in the face. "How do you figure that?"

Sam shrugged. "Well, think about it. They go to court to get the right to put ads on public buses. Just makes me think they wouldn't do something like planting a bomb."

Makayla snorted again. "They only went to court to get the publicity."

"So how does bombing a movie theater get them publicity?" Sam asked.

"What's been on the local news the past few days?" Makayla sighed ... heavy, as she rolled her eyes.

"That doesn't get any publicity for *them*."

"Maybe they didn't want publicity. Maybe this time they wanted to hurt their opposition — Christians."

"I just don't know," said Sam.

The five minute bell rang. Mrs. Forge clapped her hands. "Students, close your files, shut down the computers, and prepare your personal items for dismissal."

Makayla hit the button to shut down the system. "Want me to see what I can find on their leader tonight?"

"Sure," said Sam. "Thanks. I'm sure you'll find something. You usually do."

Makayla grinned as she turned off the computer. "That's because I'm a genius. And a ninja. I'm a ninja-genius."

"And so modest, too." Sam chuckled and pushed her chair under the table.

"Hey, I checked out your blog post right before you showed up. Did you know you have almost a hundred and fifty comments?"

Man, she'd gotten almost fifty more in what, less than an hour? "I haven't gotten a chance to look yet. Ms. Pape and Aubrey were going to answer the ones they felt they needed to, I guess. I can't wait to read

THE TROUBLE WITH RESEARCH

them." But she wanted to do it when she could take her time and enjoy the moment.

"Check when you get home," said Makayla.

The bell rang and students rushed out of the classrooms like ants toward watermelon at a fourth of July picnic.

"Text me when you're done with cheer practice." Makayla rushed toward her locker.

How was she going to make it through cheerleading practice when all she wanted to do was get home, read the comments, and do more research on the coalition?

And wouldn't Dad just love her questions tonight.

CHAPTER 7

THE CALL TO ACTION

Yes, ma'am, the same Sam Sanderson who called earlier." Sam could almost hear the sigh in the woman's voice over the phone line as she recited her cell phone number. Again. "I'm with the Robinson Senators' paper." She deliberately left out the middle school part. Maybe if they thought she was with the high school, they'd respond more favorably. "I'd like to ask Mr. Hughes just a few questions."

"I'll give him *both* of your messages as soon as he's available, Ms. Sanderson," the woman said, and not in the friendliest of tones.

"I really appreciate it. I know how busy he is and thought it might be better for Mr. Hughes if I just called instead of dropping by the theater to ask my questions."

It wasn't really a threat, because Mom always said threatening and intimidation wouldn't help secure a source, but this was just trying to get past the theater owner's personal assistant.

"I'm sure he'll appreciate that. Thank you, Ms. Sanderson. Goodbye."

The click boomed loud against Sam's ear, then the dial tone sounded.

She tossed her Bluetooth headset onto her desk and stared at her laptop screen. She paced the short space in front of her desk. The blog continued to get a steady stream of comments, all about Bobby Milner. The bombing itself seemed to get lost. She needed to get the focus back on the bombing itself. And the theater.

She needed a backup in case Mr. Hughes didn't call her back.

Her legs trembled as she paced faster. They'd had quite the workout in cheer practice today. After practice, Kate's mom had brought Sam home. Since Kate was on the squad, too, and only lived one block over, whenever they had practice and Mom was out on assignment, Kate's mom was nice enough to bring Sam home. When there was no practice, Mrs. Willis, their next-door neighbor, picked her up from school.

Sam quickly texted Makayla and asked her to see what she could find on Frank Hughes.

Her smartphone sounded the text alert almost immediately.

Sam snatched it up and opened her text from Makayla:

No net research tonight. Mom watching over my shoulder. Grr.

Great. One more avenue closed off.

No, she couldn't think that way. Mom always said, "Real journalists don't accept closed doors. We find window-ways in."

Chewy jumped off the bed, barking, scrambling toward the foyer. Dad had to be home.

Sam laughed and headed to the kitchen. She pulled out the salad mix from the refrigerator just as Dad came through the front door. His keys clanked into the wooden bowl on the entry table. Maybe she'd find her window-way in the press release Dad brought home. "Hi, Daddy," she called out.

"Hi, Sam," he said, his voice dragging. As usual, he went immediately to his room to lock his gun and badge. He came back and checked the chicken casserole in the oven. "Looks like it's ready."

She nodded. "Should be. I put it in the oven as soon as Kate's mom dropped me off after practice."

Dad grabbed the hot pads, then pulled the pan from the oven. When Mom was home, Sam would help her make up a lot of casseroles that were easy to freeze and store. That way, when Mom was gone, Sam and her dad always had home-cooked, easy-to-reheat meals.

Within minutes, Sam sat across the table from Dad, hot chicken casserole with ready-bake rolls and garden salad in front of them. Dad said a quick prayer over the food, then took a long sip of milk. Sam immediately shoveled in a bite of the casserole, then had to suck in air to cool it. Dad always picked on her about not being patient enough to let her food cool before she dug in. But he was silent now.

She studied him. Uh-oh. He wore his *bulldog* expression. And she hadn't even asked him for the press release yet.

"About the article you wrote that was posted on the school's blog today ..." He paused, setting down his glass and meeting her stare. "About Bobby Milner and his past ..."

Oh. So that's what he was upset about. "Dad, his police report is public record. Anybody with a little determination can find that information."

"The question is, how did *you*?"

She slowly swallowed the chicken casserole that now tasted like her pom-pom strings. "Did you know police reports are available online these days?" Not that *she* looked it up, but that didn't change the fact that she *could* have. "I didn't do anything wrong. I didn't make anything up. I didn't add anything to the truth. I exercised responsible reporting." How many times had she heard Mom argue for her colleagues in the same way?

"I didn't say you did anything wrong, Sam. But you

didn't give all the facts. Like Mr. Milner's *violent offense* was dropped and he hasn't had any further issue with the police," he said.

She swallowed hard, heat already crawling up the back of her neck. "Dad, *you're* the one who's argued that domestic abusers are some of the worst kinds. Are you taking up for Mr. Milner?"

Dad shook his head. "Not at all. I'm merely pointing out that you didn't give all the information you have. You can't just pick and choose what you give the public."

Why not? Isn't that what news people meant by the phrase *the slant*? Each reporter had their own take on a story, and that take was how they slanted the tone and text of their article. Dad knew all that, so why was he acting like this?

He sighed. "Since I'm the lead detective, when you write something like that, people assume your information comes from me. I can't tell you how many people asked me if Bobby Milner was my prime suspect." Dad shook his head. "Even my captain."

"Just tell them that I do my own research. I find my own story slant." Couldn't people understand she was quite capable of forming her own opinion and finding her own story details? She was getting mighty tired of everyone treating her like she was some little kid.

Dad sighed again. "It's not that easy, Sam." He finally

shoved a forkful of the casserole into his mouth and chewed.

"I didn't even use the answers you gave me in the interview. Well, except for the *no comment* part," she said, her fork hovering over her plate. Her own hunger had disappeared faster than Chewy after a squirrel.

"I just wish you'd let someone else handle this one."

What? Give away her one decent chance at making editor? *So* not happening. She shook her head. "I'm sorry, Daddy. I can't." She wouldn't. *God, please don't let him make me give this up!*

He took another bite, this time chewing so hard the little muscles in his jaw danced.

She had to make him understand how important this was to her. "It's part of my job on the school paper. You've always said I have to build strong work ethics, right?"

"This isn't what I meant, Sam," he said.

"Isn't it?" She let her fork clatter to the plate. "Daddy, I might only be in seventh grade, but you know I want to be a journalist when I grow up. Being on the school newspaper is a way of building toward my career goal." At least, that's how Mom said it when she bragged about Sam wanting to become a journalist.

"And this is a good story, real news, not some 'teacher tips'-type article. Something important." She hated that it sounded like she was begging for his permission. She wasn't.

He and Mom had agreed she could be on the newspaper. Surely he couldn't change his mind now.

Man, I wish Mom was home.

"I understand that, pumpkin, I do."

"Then what's the issue?" she asked.

He pressed his napkin to his mouth. "Because it's my case, everything I do is under scrutiny. Especially a case as important as this."

"But that's just it, Daddy. What *you* do. Not what I do."

"I'm sorry, but in this case, because you're my daughter, what you do is under scrutiny, too," he said.

Her heart pounded against her chest so hard. "So what are you saying, Daddy?" she asked. Her stomach cramped, like the chicken casserole she'd choked down wasn't going to stay down.

"I'd like you to not report on this anymore. Let someone else take this story."

No way! She'd fought Aubrey too hard to get the assignment to just give it back. Sam's mouth got drier than Mom's sense of humor. "I can't. I'm sorry, Daddy. It means too much to me." Boy, did it ever!

Neither said anything for a moment. A very long moment. Finally, Dad took a sip of milk, then set down his glass. "I won't tell you that you can't report on it. At least, not now. But, Sam, please understand the position I'm in."

Would he order her to give up the story? She wanted

to scream and rant but knew — all too well from past experience — that wouldn't work to her advantage. Instead, she took a deep breath. "I do respect you as the detective on the case, Daddy. I just ask for the same thing—respect as the reporter covering the case."

He smiled, the little lines at the corners of his eyes deep, like his eyes were weighted down. "You've got a deal, Ms. Sanderson."

● ● ●

The press release was a joke!

Sam reread it for the third time. Nothing she didn't already know was in the statement. She balled up the paper and tossed it into the trashcan. What a waste of a perfectly good press conference.

She checked the state newspaper's blog, but nothing really new had been posted about the bombing. The latest headline was about the Arkansas Razorbacks' upcoming first game. Really? She was a huge Hog fan and all, but football ousting a bombing on the news page? How messed up was that?

Her cellphone rang. She jumped, then laughed at herself as she answered. "Hello."

"Sam Sanderson?" a man's voice asked.

"This is she."

"This is Frank Hughes, returning your call."

He'd called back! Sam reached for her iPad with her

questions as she slipped onto her bed. Sitting cross-legged, she said, "Thank you for getting back with me. I'm with the Robinson Senator newspaper, and I have a few questions for you."

"Of course."

How nice was he? Her fingers poised over the iPad's keyboard. "Mr. Hughes, how long have you owned the Chenal 9 Theater?"

"Well, we opened in 2008, under the Dickinson Theatres' ownership, me being the manager. Two years later, they allowed me to purchase the theater as a franchise."

Sam typed furiously. "A franchise? How, exactly, does that work?" she asked.

"A franchise is a business system where a bigger and established company gives a person or a smaller business the rights to sell its products and to operate under its brand name. The smaller company, or person, has to operate under guidelines of the bigger company to protect the brand name."

"I see," she said, but she really didn't. She needed clarification. "So, it's kinda like you own a branch of Dickinson Theatres, but you have to operate under their rules?" she asked. At least she learned something new today.

"Right."

"That must cost a lot of money. To buy a franchise, I mean."

He didn't answer. Silence filled the phone

connection. Her heart pounded against her ribs. Just how much money did he stand to lose?

"Could they, if they had a legitimate reason, make you give back the franchise?" she asked as she popped her knuckles.

"Well, there are some very specific guidelines I must adhere to. If not, then the short answer is, yes, they could demand their branded name back."

"But you'd get to keep the theater itself, right?" she asked. Or would he lose everything?

"If I could afford it."

"Um," she scanned her list of questions. "How has this bomb affected the theater's business?"

"As you can imagine, some people are leery of coming to the theater, but I want to assure everyone that we are 100 percent safe and secure. I've hired additional security, who conduct hourly sweeps of the entire building, and we've installed video surveillance for the entire theater."

"That's a lot of expense, isn't it?" she asked.

"You can't put a price on people's safety, and I want everyone to know that," Mr. Hughes said.

Price on safety? Hmm. "Mr. Hughes, had this bomb detonated, what would have been the outcome with Dickinson in regards to your owning a franchise?"

"I don't know exactly, but don't you worry none. I carry good insurance to cover my investment."

Maybe so. Time to flip points. "Mr. Hughes, do you

have any idea who would want to put a bomb in the theater, set to detonate when a private showing had been scheduled?"

"I've given all that information to the police," he said, his tone changing to more formal-sounding. "I feel quite confident they'll find who did this and see that justice is served."

"How's that?" she asked. Had he gotten some inside information from the police that Dad hadn't shared with her?

"Excuse me?" Definitely a more formal tone.

"What makes you so confident? Did you give the police leads on who you believe is responsible for placing the bomb in the closet by the ladies' restroom?"

"Um," he paused. "Well, I just believe our police will do everything in their power to find who did this and see justice served. I'm sorry, I need to go now."

"Thank you, Mr. Hughes, for calling me back," she said just before he hung up. Last year, she'd asked Mom to share her little tidbits of how to be a great journalist. One of the things Mom told her was to always be polite and thank people when they took the time to answer questions, even if they didn't answer the way she wanted.

Sam set her phone down on the desk, staring at the notes on her iPad as if her article direction would jump up at her. She glanced up to the digital frame with Mom's articles and replayed the conversation in her mind.

Inspiration struck. She moved to the ergonomic chair in front of her desk and quickly ran an Internet search on *average cost of business security systems*. The search engine threw up over forty-six million results. She clicked on the first one that looked legit, then rubbed Chewy behind her ears while she waited for the page to load. From the informational page, she went to a pricing page for video surveillance systems and was surprised. The prices for a decent system ran anywhere from $4,000.00 to $15,000.00.

Mr. Hughes was serious about security. And that amount didn't even include the cost of paying for security guards. If he was paying out this kind of money, he really wanted people to feel safe at the movies.

Well … now that she thought about it. Sam pulled up the website for the theater, then opened the calculator app on her iPhone. Regular ticket prices were $9.25 each. On a Saturday, they ran about forty movies, not counting the special — and higher priced — IMAX showings. If just twenty people showed up for every showing, which was kind of a low estimate in Sam's opinion because she'd never seen it that slow, that was eight hundred tickets. Eight hundred at $9.25 each was $7,400.00 a day. That was a lot of money.

No wonder Mr. Hughes wanted people to feel safe enough to come back to the theater.

But she couldn't forget he hadn't commented when

she'd asked about the cost of the franchise. Nor could she forget his comment about having insurance.

What if Dickinson was about to demand the franchise back for whatever reason? He said if that happened, he could only keep the theater open if he could afford it. What if he didn't have the money?

Sam plopped back onto her bed, laying on her back and staring up at the ceiling fan. Chewy jumped up and licked her face. Sam laughed and rubbed Chewy's tummy. An idea flitted across her mind, then screeched to a halt. She bolted upright.

What if Mr. Hughes knew Dickinson was about to demand back the franchise and he couldn't afford to lose the money he'd invested — his word, not hers — so he needed to claim the insurance? Something would have to happen to the theater itself for that to happen. Sam chewed her bottom lip. What if the bomb was only meant to set fire to the theater?

She sat back in front of her desk and ran another search. This time on arson statistics.

CHAPTER 8

IMPLICATIONS AND ASSUMPTIONS

… According to a report by the US Fire Administration, arson is the leading cause of fires in the United States: over 267,000 each year. An insurance research council estimates that 14% of those arson cases were set to gain insurance money. That same report estimates that arson fires cost over 878 MILLION dollars a year.

What do YOU think? Could the bomb have been a failed arson attempt? Sound Off, Senators. Leave a comment with your thoughts. ~ Sam Sanderson, reporting

"Sam!" Ms. Pape called out as soon as Sam entered the classroom for the last period of the day.

"Yes, ma'am?" She set her books on her desk and turned.

Ms. Pape stood huddled in the corner with Aubrey and Mrs. Trees, the school principal.

Uh-oh. None of them wore a happy expression. Except maybe Aubrey. She wore a smirk, but that wasn't really anything out of the ordinary for her. Especially when it came to how she looked at Sam all the time.

Sam joined them. "Yes, ma'am?" she asked again, fixing the smile she didn't feel across her face.

"About your article in today's blog," Ms. Pape began. "The implication that Mr. Hughes might've planted the bomb himself is very clear. Was it intentional?" She clasped her hands in front of her body, her bony arms whiter than they should be in late August.

"I didn't imply Mr. Hughes had anything to do with the bomb. I stated the facts regarding arson fires, then I asked people to consider if the bomb plant might've been an attempt at arson. I never even mentioned Mr. Hughes in the last two paragraphs." Sam felt like someone had shoved cotton down the back of her throat.

"But the first two paragraphs were about Mr. Hughes and franchises," Mrs. Trees said, her penciled-in eyebrows nearly a straight line. "It's a natural progression of the article that implies Mr. Hughes could have been involved for financial reasons."

"Mrs. Trees, I apologize for not reviewing her article more closely," Ms. Pape interjected, then turned to Sam. "The implication was clear with your one question: *Could the bomb have been a failed arson attempt?*

You asked the question, putting the idea in the reader's mind. Reporters shouldn't editorialize or sensationalize. Just report the facts."

That was the whole point. "I didn't use his name. I just asked a question about it possibly being a failed arson attempt. I didn't say Mr. Hughes had been involved." Sam's mouth was totally spitless.

"Mr. Hughes called me this afternoon," Mrs. Trees said. "He's threatening to sue your parents, me, the school, the school district, Ms. Pape ... everybody who has anything to do with you and the paper for defamation of character. He said that not only did you slander his reputation, but because so many have read your article, the damage to his good name is even worse. "

Sam shook her head. She knew all too well her freedom of speech rights. That was the first rule of journalism, and Mom had told her time and again to learn the rights of journalists. *All* journalists. She licked her lips with a dry tongue. "He can't. I am protected, as is the paper, you, Ms. Pape, and the school, under the first amendment. We are protected from anyone's *abridging the freedom of speech, or of the press.*" She smiled at Aubrey. "That includes school presses." Mom would be proud — right? Sam sure was proud of herself, because she'd worked long and hard to memorize all that.

Neither Ms. Pape nor Mrs. Trees looked impressed.

"I didn't print — *Was this bomb plant Mr. Hughes' failed arson attempt?* — did I?" she asked. "No, I didn't, because that wouldn't be responsible reporting. But posing a legitimate question and making people think—that *is* responsible reporting."

Ms. Pape's lips puckered as silence held.

"That's not the point." Mrs. Trees shook her head. "I told you I wasn't sure the blog was a good idea," she told Ms. Pape. "This is a prime example why I didn't want to try it out in the first place. Not even a full week, and already I'm getting threats of being sued. I should have never allowed the blog to go up."

"Mrs. Trees, please don't punish us all for one person's mistake," Aubrey said. "I'll reassign the story to someone else."

"No!" Sam clamped her hands over her mouth. The word had slipped out before she could stop it.

Mrs. Trees, Ms. Pape, and Aubrey all stared at her as if a unicorn horn had sprouted out of her forehead.

Sam swallowed. "I meant, you shouldn't shut down the blog, Mrs. Trees. Good journalists will tell you that if the article content isn't making people stop and think, then the reporters aren't doing their jobs." She glanced at Ms. Pape. Why wasn't she chiming in here to help defend the paper's freedom of speech rights? Mom would be jumping up and down right now if she was in this meeting.

"Mr. Hughes was upset and lashed out at you, but I promise you, he has no grounds for any legitimate claim," Sam said. Neither Mrs. Trees nor Ms. Pape said a word, so maybe she'd made her point. Still, she needed to make sure. "Shutting down the blog is wrong, but so is changing anything, even reporters. To do so now would only make it appear as if we'd done something wrong." She set her jaw. "And we haven't."

Once again, silence hung as heavy over them as the sweaters Dad made Sam wear when it was just a teensy bit chilly. And it was just as hot and suffocating to her.

"Excuse me, Ms. Pape, but you need to see this," Lana Wilson said. She held up her tablet where they could see the screen. Sam's blog post page.

Just great. Sam groaned silently. Just when she'd been making her point, now her misstep was brought back front and center for them all to see again. *Oh, Lana!*

"Look at all these comments," Lana said. "And most every one of them thanks the paper and the school for making them think and consider something they hadn't before." She swiped her finger across the screen. "Like this one, from *a college student* who posts: Thank you for articles without bias and political ramifications."

Aubrey's eyes widened.

Ms. Pape took the tablet and read aloud. "From *a concerned parent* who posted: I applaud the newspaper for putting out more information than the regular newspaper. Kudos, *Senator Speak*." She scrolled further. "And another, from someone calling themselves *truth seeker* who wrote: I commend the reporter for going above and beyond in this article. Looking forward to reading the continued reports on the blog."

Aubrey's face turned a deep red.

"There are already three hundred and eight comments on the blog," Ms. Pape said as she handed the tablet back to Lana. "Thank you, Lana. I'll be with the class in a moment."

"Well," Mrs. Trees began, "I suppose I could wait a day or so to see if there's any further negative repercussions regarding this article."

"I can still stay on as the reporter, right, Ms. Pape?" Sam asked, then looked to the principal. "Okay, Mrs. Trees?"

She held her breath. If they let Aubrey give this to that jock, Kevin, Sam would scream.

Loud and long.

Ms. Pape gave Sam a weak smile. "For now, yes."

Yes! Sam nodded.

"I know you're the editor, Aubrey, but for now, Sam stays as the reporter on this assignment," Ms. Pape said. Her tone didn't allow room for any argument.

By the look on Aubrey's face, it looked like she really wanted to argue about it too. She wisely stayed silent.

"You girls join the class. I'll be there in a moment," Ms. Pape said, turning to face Mrs. Trees.

It was all Sam could do not to skip over to where Lana and Celeste huddled over the tablet, reading the blog comments.

"You might think you've won this round, Samantha

Sanderson, but you'd better be very careful. I'm looking for a reason to have you kicked off the paper. Permanently," Aubrey said with that smirky smile of hers as Nikki rushed to stand beside her.

Sam smiled back, and in the sweetest voice she could muster, answered, "I expect no less, Aubrey. You've been trying to do that since I signed on. Why should now be any different?"

Aubrey narrowed her eyes. "I'm confident you'll mess up again real soon, so I'm not worried that I'll have to put up with you much longer." She flipped her dirty blond hair over her shoulder and headed to the editor's desk, then sat, still glaring at Sam.

Nikki hesitated, then followed in Aubrey's wake.

Sam shook her head and moved away.

"Don't mind her. She just drank a double dose of hater-aide today," said Lana, catching her shoulder-length brown hair into a ponytail and securing it with a scrunchie.

Sam grinned and plopped into the empty chair beside Celeste. "I wish I knew what I'd done to make her hate me."

"She's probably just jealous," Celeste said, mocking, as she flipped her auburn hair in Aubrey's dramatic way.

"Yeah." Lana made a duck-face. "Cuz you're so smart and all." She batted her eyes, fluttering her long eyelashes.

Sam and Celeste laughed.

"And because you're a better journalist than her." Lana pointed at the tablet. "Now you're up to three hundred and thirty-one comments. All commending your article and you."

Sam scrolled to read random students' comments: "Good job," "keep up the great reporting," and so on. She felt like her heart could explode at any minute. She'd have to text Mom the link when she got home from school.

"Good article, Sam," Luke Jensen said. He gave Sam's arm a mock punch as he passed them on the way to his desk.

Words failed Sam as her heart raced, and her face went hotter than an August afternoon in Arkansas.

Both Lana and Celeste stared after him until he plopped in a seat at the table with the rest of the guys on the paper's staff, then looked back at Sam. Their eyes were wide. Then all three girls burst into giggles.

Ohmygummybears! Ohmygummybears! Ohmygummybears! Just wait until she told Makayla that Luke Jensen not only remembered her name but had read her article. AGAIN!

Sam finished entering the link for the school paper's blog, then sent the text to her mom. There were now over three hundred and sixty comments, and most all of them were still really positive. At least about Sam and her reporting. Some people had speculated about Frank Hughes being involved with the bomb, but Sam didn't think so.

It didn't make sense for him to plant a bomb where someone could find it so easily. He owned the place ... had to know about every little hiding space there was, so surely he'd have put a bomb where no one would find it before it went off. He wouldn't have been so stupid as to have put it in the supply closet by the restroom.

Well, the theater employee *did* say they'd already concluded their nightly closing procedures in that area. Even so, Mr. Hughes hadn't been at the theater that night. At least, that's what he said. Sam believed him. She'd only written the article to make people think. To consider all options.

To keep seeking until the truth came out.

That was Mom's motto. Now it was Sam's, too.

Chewy's barking echoed outside. Oh, bullies! She'd forgotten to let the dog back inside, and now Dad was home. He'd lecture her, again, about leaving Chewy outside too long in the heat.

Sam rushed to the backdoor and let Chewy in. The dog went and gulped at her water bowl. Sam refilled it with cold water, then checked the lasagna in the oven. It wasn't bubbling yet. She'd forgotten to put it in the oven as soon as she'd gotten home. Great, something else for Dad to talk to her about.

She grabbed the salad mix and dumped it into two bowls, rushing. Maybe he wouldn't realize she'd been late starting dinner. The lasagna pan was pretty deep … maybe he'd think it just took longer to heat.

The front door clicked shut. Oops, she'd forgotten to lock it. Dad would have plenty to talk with her about tonight. His keys clanked into the wooden bowl on the entry table.

Maybe she should get the jump on his mood. "Hi, Daddy," she called out, sounding as happy as she felt. After all, she was on top of the world. Her article was getting some amazing responses, Ms. Pape hadn't let Aubrey take the assignment away from her, and Luke Jensen had been impressed with her article.

His footsteps seemed to drag as he came out of his bedroom and into the kitchen. He looked so drained.

"Sit down, Daddy. The lasagna isn't ready just yet. We can start on our salads, though." Sam put their glasses of tea on the placemats. She put the salad bowls there while Dad plopped into his chair.

He offered up grace as soon as she sat, then reached for his tea. Must have had a really awful day. She felt a little guilty since her day had been nearly perfect. She didn't want to ask him how his day had gone, but it seemed rude not to. "How was your day?" she asked.

He straightened his plate on the placemat, then aligned his fork on the napkin beside the plate. Uh-oh, a sure sign he was planning how to say something. If he had to plan, it had to be bad. "My captain received a call from Frank Hughes today." Dad stared at her, making her want to squirm.

She resisted the urge. Instead, she squared her shoulders. "I already spoke with both Ms. Pape and Mrs. Trees, Daddy. I explained about a journalist's freedom of speech and — "

"I know where you're going, Sam. I'm not talking about your freedom of speech," Dad interrupted, holding up his hand. "My point is, I need to know where you're getting your information."

"Wh-what? Mr. Hughes spoke to me on the phone. I have my notes, Dad. I didn't make anything up. I can show you." She stood, nearly knocking over her chair.

"Sit down. I don't need to see your notes. I believe you," said Dad. He continued to ignore his bowl of salad before him.

She slipped back down into her chair. "That's the only place I got my information. Well, I got the numbers about arson off the Internet."

"Let me ask it another way: Why would you focus your article on Frank Hughes and arson attempts?" Dad asked.

Sam explained how she'd gone from learning about franchises to researching the cost of security systems, to remembering what Mr. Hughes had said about insurance, to researching that angle. "Why?"

The bulldog look filled Dad's face. "This is totally off the record, Samantha. I mean it."

Her heart caught in her chest. She hated to be called Samantha and Dad knew that, so he had to be really serious. All she could do was nod.

"Because early this morning, we received a copy of the insurance policy Mr. Hughes has on the theater." Dad took a sip of tea. It felt to Sam like he drank in slow motion before he set his glass back on the table. "While his policy has standard and acceptable amounts of liability coverage, he's carrying an exorbitantly high amount of property coverage. Almost three times more than what our insurance specialists recommend."

Three times? That was a lot. A *whole* lot.

"So, you see why my captain is asking how, last night, before we received copies of the insurance policies, you were able to pose the question of attempted arson for insurance fraud."

Sam's pulse spiked. She'd actually been a step *ahead* of the investigation. Wow.

This was better than Luke Jensen's attention. *Hello, editor. Here I come.*

CHAPTER 9

UNBURYING THE PAST

"You are not going to believe this," Makayla's voice sounded even more animated over the phone headset snuggled against Sam's ear. "Oh, hang on."

Muffled sounds came from Makayla's end. Voices. Makayla's mom.

Sam tapped her fingernail against her tablet. She sat cross legged on her bed, staring at how cute Chewy looked curled into a ball at the foot of the bed. Her iPad's notes section was open in front of her as she tried to think of what she could write for her next article.

Dad had all but ordered her to not mention Frank Hughes in her next article. That was okay with her: she needed something new and fresh for tomorrow anyway.

And it made it seem like she wanted to do what Dad asked, which she did—most times.

"Sorry, Mom is breathing down my neck again," Makayla said. "I'm back now."

"What is up with your mom?"

"I don't know. It's like all of a sudden, she's phased into nosy-ninja-mom."

"Is she still going to let you go to Playtime Pizza with me on Saturday?"

"She hasn't said anything about cancelling, so we're still on," Makayla said.

"So, what am I not going to believe?" Sam had never been big on patience. Ever. Sometimes — too many times for Sam's liking — Makayla got sidetracked. Sam had to keep her best friend on track.

"I was finally able to do some research on Jessica Townsend."

The spokesperson of the local chapter of the Central Arkansas Coalition of Reason. Finally. "And?" Sam sat upright. *Come on, Mac—just spit it out!*

Chewy lifted her head and stared at Sam with her big, chocolate eyes before settling her head back down on the bed.

"Well, for all her proclamations that we don't need God, she was raised a Christian. Her family still attends church twice weekly."

"Hmm," Sam said. That was interesting, but not

really something useful to tie into the story. She needed something more. Something meaty.

"That's not all," said Makayla. "I'm pretty certain the Jessica Townsend who is so vocal about being anti-God is the same Jessica Townsend who lived in a local convent from the time she was seventeen until she was twenty-two. At that age, according to the records I've found, Jessica attacked one of the nuns and then was sent to a psychiatric hospital for assessment and treatment."

This was interesting. "She attacked a nun?" Sam asked, typing a note. *Who in their mind attacks a nun?*

"Yes. And was sent to a hospital for individuals with mental illness who have allegedly committed a crime. For about eighteen months."

"And after eighteen months, she was all cured of crazy?"

Makayla chuckled. "I don't know. I can't get to those records. At least, not from here."

"Are you sure it's her?" Sam asked as stared at the cursor on the tablet.

"Ninety-nine percent."

This could be really good. Who attacks a nun, of all people? "What hospital?" Sam asked Makayla.

"Arkansas State Hospital. Right here in Little Rock."

Interesting. She typed the name of it in her notes. "Makayla, before I can print this, I need to verify it's the same Jessica Townsend."

"I'm on it. I'll call you back." Makayla hung up

quickly, the sounds of her typing on her keyboard already pecking away in the background.

If Jessica Townsend was crazy enough to attack a nun and get sent to a nuthouse, then she could easily be crazy enough to plant a bomb.

Can't write about Frank Hughes, no worries. Jessica Townsend's crazy past was a window-way in.

Her cell rang. Sam clicked the Bluetooth headset on without even looking at the caller-ID on the phone. "That was fast, Mac," she said as she uncrossed her legs and stretched them out on the bed.

"That's because I'm not Makayla."

"Mom!" Sam smiled.

"Hey there, my girl. How are you?"

"Good. Did you get my text?" Sam asked.

"I did. And I was able to check out the blog for a few minutes. Well done, Sam. I'm proud of you."

Sam's face could split because she smiled so wide. Heat flamed her face. "Aw, thanks, Mom."

"I mean it, Sam. You're really showing off that talent I already knew you had."

Words wouldn't even form.

"So, tell me how upset Ms. Pape and Mrs. Trees were," Mom said.

"How'd you know?" Sam asked.

"Because when people get uncomfortable, they call the editor-in-chief. Since you write for a school paper, they'd call the principal, who would bring in the news-paper's sponsoring teacher."

"You're right. At first, Mrs. Trees was furious. She said Mr. Hughes called and threatened to sue everybody, but I was quick to tell her that he couldn't because of journalists' freedom of speech rights."

"Be very careful, Sam. Even most journalists don't truly have a grasp on freedom of speech," Mom said.

"Well, once she read the comments, she backed off." Sam rested her head against the wooden headboard. "Aubrey wanted to take the story away from me, but I argued not to change a thing. Ms. Pape backed me up."

"That's great. It was a good article, honey, but I do want you to be very careful in your reporting. Slander and malice are serious stuff. Just be careful to stick only to the facts in your future articles, and no outright implications." Mom paused for a minute. "I talked to Dad. He said you agreed not to write another article about the theater owner. Are you okay with that?"

Just like Mom to understand the situation from a journalist's point of view. Sam smiled and drew her knees to her chest. "Yeah. I have to go at it from differ-ent angles anyway. Keep it fresh. Original."

"Got an idea for your next article?" Mom asked.

She glanced at the notes she'd scribbled. "Yeah, I think so. I'm waiting on Makayla to call me back. She's verifying something for me."

"You mean she's looking up something on the

computer she's not supposed to?" Mom asked, but her tone was still light.

Sam gave a little laugh. It wasn't really a secret that there wasn't much Makayla couldn't uncover on a computer. Mom understood. "Maybe."

"I've got to go, sweetheart. Stay out of trouble. And Mac, too."

"We will."

"I'll check the blog tomorrow and read your article. Goodnight, my girl. I love you lots."

"I love you, too, Mom. Goodnight."

Sam tapped the button on the headset to disconnect the call. Just hearing Mom tell her she was proud of her made Sam's heart stutter. Her dreams were finally coming true.

The call indicator buzzed in her ear. She pressed the button. "Hello?"

"Hey. It's me," Makayla said. "I can only talk for a second. Mom's on her ninja-nosy-mom routine again."

"Well?"

"It's her. The same Jessica Townsend."

"You're sure?" Sam asked.

"I'm positive. Oh, and I have some queries on Frank Hughes for you, but right now, I gotta go. Talk to you tomorrow."

Sam tossed the headset onto the bed and let out a little whoop. Chewy jumped up, clearly not pleased with Sam disturbing her, then circled twice before laying back down.

She didn't care. She had her angle for tomorrow's article. Mom would *really* be proud when she read it.

● ● ●

… Even professionals in the mental health community can't dispute the facts. The founder of the Mental Illness Policy Org. said that some mass killers "were seen by mental health professionals who did not have to report their illness or that they were becoming dangerous and they went on to kill."

What do YOU think? Could someone who previously attacked a *nun* and was sent to a state mental hospital be capable of planting a bomb as some sort of anti-religion statement? Sound Off, Senators. Leave a comment with your thoughts. ~ Sam Sanderson, reporting

"You've gone too far this time, Samantha Sanderson," Aubrey said as soon as Sam entered the cafeteria. She stood with her arms crossed, Nikki at her side.

Every morning, students who arrived at least ten minutes before school began had to wait in the cafeteria. Most of them came early on purpose — to visit with their friends. Sam always had to wait on Makayla, who rode a bus and often only had a few minutes to catch up before the bell rang.

Luckily, today wasn't one of those days, and Makayla came up to join Sam in facing Aubrey and Nikki.

"What are you blabbering about, Aubrey?" Sam asked. She set her backpack on a table and put her hands on her hips.

"Your article this morning. Mrs. Trees has already been in here looking for you. I'm sure she and Ms. Pape are going to kick you off the paper today. You should be very worried." Aubrey's smirk seemed more evil today. "It's like Christmas, only early."

"I find it amusing that you, the editor, are kept out of the loop," Sam said. "Maybe you're the one who should be worried."

Aubrey's face stiffened. She opened her mouth —

"Sam Sanderson," Mrs. Trees called out.

Sam turned. The principal waved her over. Mrs. Trees wore a strict expression. Ever her hair looked harsh.

Aubrey flashed her a fake smile. "Yeah, bye-bye. You're outta my hair." She waved with her fingers before flipping her hair and flouncing off toward a group of eighth graders. Nikki scrambled to keep up.

Great. She probably was a goner. Sam grabbed her backpack.

Makayla gave her a quick side-hug. "It'll be okay. I'll be praying," she whispered, ever the optimist.

Feeling as if she were being led to certain death, Sam

dragged her feet as she crossed the cafeteria toward the principal.

"My office. Now," Mrs. Trees said as she led the way from the cafeteria.

Tap-tap-tap, the principal's heels echoed off the painted concrete. Wind pushed down the open corridor as they passed the counselor's office. A hint of beans filled the air, a warning of what would be served for lunch today.

Tap. Tap.

Another blast of hot air surged down the breezeway. Sam's hair blew across her face. She grabbed the thick length and wound it around her hand, holding it. In front of her, Mrs. Trees had no problem. Her hair was probably too scared to move out of place even in a tornado.

Tap. Tap. Tap. Tap.

Mrs. Trees turned the corner. Students hung out around the front of the office. "Aren't you children supposed to be in the cafeteria until the bell rings?" the principal asked. "I suggest you get where you belong."

The kids scattered. Some of them tossed Sam looks of pity as they passed. Her stomach free-fell to her toes. Aubrey was right — she was going to be kicked off the paper.

Her legs were lead weights as she followed Mrs. Trees into the office and down the hall. The carpet muffled the principal's steps, but it still felt like a death march to Sam.

She followed Mrs. Trees into the principal's office, not surprised to find Ms. Pape sitting in one of the chairs in front of the desk. A witness to her humiliation.

"Please, sit down," said Mrs. Trees as she sat behind her desk.

As if she had a choice? Sam sat in the only empty chair in the office.

"Now, about your article this morning," Mrs. Trees began.

"I promise everything in there is the truth, Mrs. Trees. I didn't make any of it up. I even had — "

"Did you just interrupt me?"

Sam opened her mouth, then stopped mid-word. She clamped her mouth shut and nodded. Was she not going to be given a chance to defend herself?

"As I was saying," Mrs. Trees continued, "about your article. It's well written, indeed. I'm sure a lot of research went into it as well."

Sam pinched her lips together. Maybe this wasn't goodbye.

"Having said that, however," Mrs. Trees stared directly into Sam's eyes, "there are several students in this school who are diagnosed with what is referred to as mental illness. Some parents may take objection to some of the statements in your article."

Sam kept quiet. This wasn't the best time to argue. Not until she heard what would come next.

"It was my decision to have your blog article taken down."

What? "You-you-you can't do that." This couldn't be happening!

Mrs. Trees smiled, as if she were posing for a picture. "Oh, I can. And I did. I have to make decisions based upon what I think is best for the majority of the student body."

"The majority of the student body has been diagnosed with a mental illness?" Sure, her response could be taken as being disrespectful, but no more disrespectful than having her article killed.

The smile slipped off Mrs. Trees's face. "No, but I won't have even a handful insulted. It's almost a form of bullying."

And the entire state school system had a no-tolerance policy for any form of bullying.

"But, Mrs. Trees, the article — "

"I've made my decision, and it's final," Mrs. Trees said.

"You aren't being taken off the assignment, Sam," Ms. Pape said. "Just this one article isn't going to run on the blog."

That was little consolation. "But it was set to post early this morning." She'd set it to go live at six a.m. It had to have gone up for Mrs. Trees to see it.

Ms. Pape nodded. "It did. But we removed it about thirty minutes ago."

"Your next article can be posted as usual. Your posting abilities haven't been suspended," Ms. Pape said.

As if that made pulling this one okay?

Sam couldn't explain how sick to her stomach she felt. Mom wouldn't get to read it online. She was in another country on assignment, and it was the middle of the night where she was.

It just wasn't fair.

CHAPTER 10

A MATTER OF PRIDE

I 'm sorry they took down your blog post," Makayla said as Sam shoved her books into her locker. "It's a bummer."

Sam slammed the door and spun the lock. "It's not fair." She led the way toward the cafeteria. The smell of French fries welcomed them, but even their enticement couldn't pull her from her lousy mood.

"At least you weren't taken off the story, and you can write another article for tomorrow."

"It's not the same," Sam mumbled. "The article this morning was better than just good; it was pretty awesome. And now no one, not even Mom, will get to see it."

"I'll check all my resources and queries this afternoon when I get home. Maybe I'll have something great for you to write about tomorrow."

Sam forced a smile. "Thanks, Mac." It wasn't Makayla's fault. Her best friend was doing everything she could to cheer Sam up. Mac was the best bestie ever.

"Hey, guess what?" Lana asked as she joined Sam and Makayla, her green eyes bigger than normal.

"I can't take any more bad news," said Sam.

Lana laughed. "It's great news, actually."

"Aubrey quit the paper?" Sam gave her first real smile since leaving the principal's office.

"We couldn't get that lucky." Lana tossed her arm over Sam's shoulders. "So that's not it. No, I heard even though they killed your blog post before eight this morning, it already had like almost fifty comments."

Sam stopped moving forward in the lunch line and stared at Lana. "Are you serious?"

Lana nodded. "I only had time to read about the first twenty or so on my mom's iPhone before I had to get out of the car this morning, but those that I read were all great. Said you were digging deeper and all that stuff."

"Wow! I wish I'd seen them." *At least then I could've told Mom about them.*

"You still can," Makayla said.

"How?" Sam asked.

"Come on, girls, stop holding up the line," said Mr. Emmitt, the science teacher. He motioned them to move faster.

Once the three of them got their trays and sat down, Makayla blessed the food for them.

"So, how can I see the comments?" Sam asked. She stabbed her straw into her carton of chocolate milk.

"Well, every time a comment is posted on the blog, an email is sent to the blog's email address. In this case, Ms. Pape's." Makayla shrugged. "Just ask Ms. Pape to put all the comments into a document and then you have them all."

"How do you know this? You aren't even on the paper," Lana said.

Makayla ducked her head. "Updating the school's website is one of my EAST group projects. Today, we updated to include the paper's blog. I had to go pull the address to post and noticed the settings." She shrugged, but Sam could tell she was a little embarrassed.

"That would be great," Sam said. "If I could just get Ms. Pape to do that for me."

"Why wouldn't she?" Makayla asked.

"She's trying to make that whole post disappear, so she probably deleted all the emails." Sam shoved a fry into her mouth.

"Didn't you say that Mrs. Trees was the one who pulled the post? If Ms. Pape wasn't the one behind it, maybe she kept the emails."

Sam pushed her uneaten chicken sandwich across the plate. She ate another fry. "Maybe, but I doubt it. If Mrs. Trees told her to take down my article, then I'll bet Ms. Pape deleted the emails, too."

Makayla swiped the paper napkin across her mouth.

"Just because you delete something doesn't mean it's gone."

Sam swallowed and stared at her bestie, raising a single brow. She hadn't thought about that, but Mac was right.

"Really?" Lana asked.

Makayla lifted a casual shoulder. "It's easy enough to retrieve emails you thought you'd deleted."

"Even if you've cleared your trash out?" Lana asked.

Makayla nodded. "It's not that difficult. Most people can do it, even if they aren't all that computer savvy."

"I didn't know that." Lana looked at Sam. "Do you know how to do it?"

Sam grinned. "I do." She pointed at Makayla. "But Mac ... well, girl, you're just so ninja-good it's scary."

Makayla blushed under her light, mocha skin. "Whatever."

"Oh look, it's poor little Sa-man-tha Sanderson. Reporter wannabe." Aubrey and Nikki walked past. Aubrey suddenly stopped beside their table, almost causing Nikki to run into her. "How does it feel to be booted?"

Sam's blood boiled. She hated that Aubrey knew she detested her full name. The mean girl never failed to use it. All. The. Time. She shook her head and plastered on a wide smile. "Poor Aubrey Damas. Editor wannabe. How does it feel to be kept out of the loop?"

Aubrey's eyes narrowed into little slits. Her fists popped to her hips covered in the most expensive pair of khaki-colored jeans. "Your article was taken down this morning."

"Yep, it was. For reasons Mrs. Trees and Ms. Pape explained to me. I would enlighten you, but since neither of them felt compelled to fill you in, maybe they don't want you to know." Sam flipped her hair over her shoulder, mimicking Aubrey. "But don't worry, I'm still on the *Senator Speak*."

Aubrey's face went so many shades of red, it looked like she might burst into a fiery explosion any second. She turned and stomped off without another word, Nikki double-stepping to keep up.

The bell rang, and the cafeteria became crowded as everyone stood and made their way to the trashcans and door.

Sam held Makayla's arm, letting Lana and the others from their table go ahead of them. "Can you get into the system and retrieve those emails?" she whispered as they waited for other kids to exit first.

Makayla caught her bottom lip between her teeth. "I can."

"Will you?" Sam hated to ask, but she really wanted to read the comments, and she didn't have any classes left where she'd have access to the system. "Please?"

Makayla hesitated.

Kids pushed around them, a couple accidentally bumping into them. They were moved into the crowd and out the door. The air hot whipped around the building, shoving against them.

"Let me see how the server is set up for the paper's blog," said Makayla. "If I can get the comments without going through Ms. Pape's email, then I'll pull them into a document and email it to you."

Sam hugged her. "Thanks, Mac. I owe you." She spun the lock on her locker.

"Only if I can get them like that. I'm not going through a teacher's email. Deleted or otherwise." Makayla's face was stern as she opened her own locker.

"Right. Of course."

Sam could barely contain herself all through the afternoon periods until school dismissed. After school, she waited by the lockers again for Makayla. Newspaper had been brutal. Aubrey acting like she was somebody important as she explained why Sam's article wasn't on the blog. She hadn't said anything about comments. Nor had Ms. Pape.

Was praying that Makayla had accessed the comments wrong? Sam didn't see how. Ms. Martha always said that God knew your thoughts ... so it shouldn't be wrong that she prayed for Makayla to get copies of the comments. At least she was up front and honest, right?

"Hey." Makayla opened her locker.

"Well?" Sam asked, shifting her backpack to her shoulder. "Could you get the comments?"

Makayla smiled. "I could. I emailed them to you.

They were sitting where I could easily grab them without getting into any trouble."

Sam hugged her. "Thank you, Mac. You're the best."

Makayla giggled. "Check your email when you get
home. And I'll see if anything came back on my queries
after karate class."

"Thanks. Call me." Sam turned and headed to the car
rider line, looking for Mrs. Willis' old car. She still hated
that Dad wouldn't be able to pick her up from school the
rest of the week, so their next-door neighbor would, but
cheerleading practice wasn't held on Wednesdays, Thurs-
days, or Fridays. Usually there was a game on Thursday or
Friday. Their first game would be Friday.

Sam liked their neighbor Mrs. Willis for the most part,
even if she was hard of hearing and didn't see as well as
she used to. It was just that some of the kids who didn't
know Sam saw her getting into Mrs. Willis's old, beat-up
car and assumed Mrs. Willis was Sam's grandmother. It
was kinda embarrassing sometimes, but the only other
option was to ride a bus. And there was no way she was
doing that. Those things didn't have air conditioning,
so everybody either got their hair all blown crazy from
the windows being down or they got all hot and sweaty.
Gross. Sure, Dad refused to let her ride a bus because
they didn't have seatbelts, but that was beside the point.

She saw Mrs. Willis in the parking lot. Thankfully, in
the back row.

"Hello, dear. How was your day?" Mrs. Willis asked as Sam slid into the front seat.

The cracked vinyl nearly scorched Sam through her jeans. "Fine." There was no reason to be rude. "Thank you for picking me up."

Mrs. Willis started the car, revving the engine like she always did. Sam suspected she needed to do that to make sure the car was running. "It's no problem. I enjoy spending time with you."

Sam smiled, but her heart sat like lead in her chest. When was the last time she'd gone next door just to visit with Mrs. Willis? She couldn't remember. Was it two weeks ago, when she'd seen Mrs. Willis working in her flower beds? Mrs. Willis's husband died about three years ago. She was probably really lonely since her kids didn't live in town.

Sam made chit-chat with Mrs. Willis all the way home, but declined her offer of cookies as they pulled into her driveway. "I've got to get homework done and our casserole in the oven so it'll be hot by the time Dad gets home."

"Okay, dear. Remember, if you need anything, I'm right next door." Mrs. Willis unlocked the car door.

Without a reason, Sam reached over and hugged the older woman. "Thanks, Mrs. Willis. I'll see you later."

Sam sprinted across the yard to her garage door. She punched in the code on the keypad, and the mechanical door loudly opened. She gave Mrs. Willis a wave goodbye before heading into the house, hitting the button to shut the garage door on her way into the kitchen.

Chewy met her as soon as she walked inside, jumping and wagging her tail so hard that her whole body shivered.

Sam laughed, dropping her backpack onto the entry bench and then bending over to love on her dog. Chewy licked her face while standing on her hind legs.

She took off her student ID badge and shoved it inside her backpack before heading into the kitchen. After she let the dog into the backyard, she opened the freezer and stared inside. What casserole to have tonight?

Chili ... ugh, too hot for chili. Mexican casserole? Nah, wasn't in the mood. Finally she decided on beef noodle casserole and pulled it out. It would only take about forty-five minutes to heat to where the cheese bubbled.

She set the temperature and the timer on the oven, stuck the casserole inside, and set a can of green beans on the counter. Dinner the easy-peasy way.

Sam let the dog back in, refilled her water bowl, then grabbed her backpack and headed to her room. She opened her MacBook, then her email. Within seconds, she had Makayla's email with the document attached.

Several comments must have been between the time Lana checked and when Mrs. Trees killed the blog post because there were sixty-one comments. As Lana had stated, most of them were amazingly congratulatory on the article itself and of her as a reporter.

Only a few of them chastised her for being critical

of mental illness. One person, in fact, posted, "A person can no more help that they're mentally ill than a person can help having heart disease."

Well … true. Sam popped her knuckles and read the rest of the comments. The heart disease one was the harshest. Maybe Mrs. Trees had done the right thing to kill the post.

She reduced the file down and went back to her inbox. There was another one from Makayla. The subject line read: Hughes info. Sam opened it and read.

> I'll look for more on this after Mom leaves for ladies group. She's monitoring me again, but we are still on for Saturday. Anyway, I thought you might like to know this info: Frank Hughes lost his seventeen-year-old daughter, Trish, two years ago following a car accident. His daughter, who reportedly had only been out of a drug rehab program for a few months, ran a red light. She was killed instantly, as was the man whom she hit, Mr. Needles. Trish was the only child Frank and his wife had. Unconfirmed reports that she had drugs in her system at the time of the accident.

How horrible. Now Sam felt bad about her article. Had she only made the poor man's suffering worse? What if people stayed away from the theater and he lost so much business that he lost the franchise? He'd be bankrupt. If that happened, would she be partially responsible?

God, please forgive me if I hurt this man who recently lost so much.

CHAPTER 11

WINDOW-WAY IN

I know, Sam, but it's a little different with a school newspaper. Especially middle school," Mom said. "I know that doesn't make you feel any better, but surely you can understand where Mrs. Trees was coming from."

"I do." She already felt guilty about Mr. Hughes ... was she supposed to feel sorry for Jessica Townsend now too?

"Mom, someone's responsible for planting that bomb. I can't hold back information in my articles just because I sympathize with the potential suspects."

"Of course not. I wouldn't." Mom paused. "But you have to balance the information you give with the possibility of repercussions that can be detrimental to the people you're reporting to."

"You always said as long as the truth is reported ..."

"Yes," Mom interrupted, "but the points of mental illness aren't imperative to your story or to casting questions about the suspect."

Sam kept quiet, thinking about that. It wasn't?

"Go at it from a different angle, my girl. I know you can figure it out."

Maybe she could. "Thanks, Mom."

"I talked to Dad earlier." A long pause followed. Like she was waiting for Sam to take the conversation.

"He told you he wants me to give up the story, didn't he?" Sam asked. Surely Mom couldn't agree with him!

"He did, but I explained how important this was to you."

"Thanks, Mom. I knew you'd understand."

"I do, and you know I support you. So does your father. Just ..." Mom sounded so sad all of a sudden. "Well, cut Dad a little slack, will you? He's having a difficult time being the lead on the case, and his captain's son goes to your school. Every article you write, the son goes to the dad and asks why you know these things and he doesn't, since he's the captain's son and all."

She'd forgotten that Doug York had transferred to her school this year. He'd been attending one of the popular private schools, but rumor was he'd gotten expelled, so his dad had made him go to the public school in the district.

"Dad understands your drive, Sam, he really does. He

supports your desire to be a journalist, and he's proud of you too. He's just in a hard spot," Mom said. "So, as a favor to me, give him a little more understanding. It's hard for him. And try to find a different angle for your next article. You're talented enough that you can think outside the box. Can you please do that for me?"

Doug York *was* a big whiner. Everybody at school knew that. She didn't want Dad caught in a bad spot because of her. "Okay. I will."

"Thank you, Sam. Listen, I have to run, but I should be home next Wednesday. I'll see you then. Love you."

"I love you, too, Mom." Sam disconnected the call and set her iPhone on the desk before turning her attention back to her computer monitor.

The blinking cursor on the screen seemed to mock her. She needed something new—a fresh angle, like Mom had suggested. *What to write ... what to write ... what to write?*

Hmm. A different angle, Mom had said. A different angle.

There was no different angle. Jessica Townsend was a legitimate suspect. That she hit a nun kinda made it clear she didn't hold religion as anything sacred.

Wait a minute ... Mom said that Jessica Townsend's stay in a mental hospital wasn't important to the story.

● ● ●

... Jessica Townsend, the spokesperson of the local chapter, was the one who headed up the federal case for the right to plaster Godless ads on local Little Rock buses.

What do YOU think? Could someone who personally attacked a *nun* and professionally led the way for slamming Christianity be capable of planting a bomb as some sort of anti-religion statement? Sound Off, Senators. Leave a comment with your thoughts. ~ Sam Sanderson, reporting

"I totally didn't mention a thing about her past mental health issues," Sam said, crossing her arms over her chest as she stared at Ms. Pape. "That's what Mrs. Trees had an issue with." She ignored the victorious sneer Aubrey wore.

"I know that." Ms. Pape tapped her front teeth with the end of her pen. "It's just in this article, you all but say if Jessica Townsend could hit a nun and spearhead the bus ads, she could plant a bomb."

"But I don't say that. I *ask* that." There was nothing wrong with asking the question aloud, right? Sam knew she was skirting the very edge of a gray issue. She also knew she'd slammed Jessica Townsend for exercising her freedom of speech rights. But it was all in the name of good reporting.

At least that's what she believed.

"It should be edited." The teacher looked at Aubrey.

Sam couldn't let Aubrey cut her article, which was what her version of editing would be. "Ms. Pape, it's a fact that she assaulted a nun — it's in the court record of her case. It's also a fact that she was the leader in going into federal court to enforce her constitutional free speech rights."

"I didn't say you didn't provide facts in the article, Sam. I'm just not sure if we should leave it up in its entirety, considering her mental illness past. As you said, she's already led the way into a federal courtroom."

"And because of that, we should leave the article up." Sam tugged her hair behind her ear. "She can't have it both ways, Ms. Pape. If she is such a strict believer and supporter of freedom of speech, then she can't get mad or threaten to sue me because I exercised my exact same rights."

Ms. Pape looked at Aubrey again. "I'm going to let you make the call on editing this, Aubrey. This is what editors have to face … these kinds of decisions and consequences of their decisions."

"As much as I hate to agree with Samantha, I have to." Aubrey looked like she'd just swallowed a bug.

What? Aubrey *agreed* with her? Were the planets in some strange alignment? Was the apocalypse around the corner?

"Okay, then. I'll let it stay unless Mrs. Trees orders it taken down." Ms. Pape waved at them. "Go ahead and get to class. If you hurry you won't be late. I don't want to write either of you a pass."

Sam snatched up her backpack and slung it over her

shoulder. She followed Aubrey into the hall. "Thanks for backing me in there."

Aubrey spun and faced her. "I didn't back you in there. I made a decision for the paper, the best choice. It had nothing to do with you, I assure you, Samantha Sanderson." She marched off toward her locker just as the first bell sounded.

Hurrying, Sam barely made it to first period before the tardy bell rang. She slipped into her seat and opened her English notebook.

After Mrs. Beach had passed out their worksheets, Sam felt someone tapping her shoulder.

"So? Is your blog post going to stay up?" Grace Brannon whispered. While not in newspaper with Sam, she was a fellow cheerleader. Sam liked Grace with her bubbly personality and freckle-covered, smiling face.

"For now." Unless Mrs. Trees had already ordered Ms. Pape to take it down. Surely Ms. Pape would explain to the principal why it was okay to leave it up.

"I think the Townsend woman is behind the bombing. My mom thinks so, too, after reading your article this morning. She said she'd met Jessica Townsend at a rally or something, and Mom said she acted like a zealot or something," Grace said, keeping her voice low so Mrs. Beach wouldn't call them out.

"Really?"

Grace nodded. "Mom said she went to one of those coalition meetings and thought it was more about bashing Christians than anything else." She shrugged and sat back in her chair.

Why would Grace's mom go to such a meeting? Grace didn't attend Sam's church, but that didn't mean she didn't attend *a* church.

But why would a Christian attend one of the Coalition of Reason meetings? It made no sense. Unless it was to get information for a news article, but Grace's mom wasn't a journalist. Was she?

Sam turned and whispered to Grace, "What does your mom do?"

"She doesn't do anything but stay at home. Why?"

Sam shrugged. "Just wondered why she'd go to one of those meetings."

"Because she thought it was a group who would help non-believers realize there's a community for them not governed by biblical faiths," said Grace.

"Oh." Sam turned back to her worksheet. Heat fanned her face, but no more than burned in her chest.

Did that mean, like she thought it did, that Grace's mom wasn't a Christian? Did that mean Grace wasn't either? Sam didn't know if she'd ever really known a non-Christian.

And she didn't know how to feel about it.

Sam tried to concentrate on the worksheet, but her mind wouldn't shut up long enough. She couldn't imagine not being a Christian. She knew not everyone had accepted Jesus into their hearts, but she just couldn't understand why not.

How could anyone refuse salvation? It just made no sense at all.

Grace poked Sam's shoulder. Sam turned around.

"What's the deal?" Grace asked.

"About what?"

"You curled up your lip when I told you why my mom went to that meeting."

"I didn't."

"Yeah, you did," Grace said. "Do you have a problem with that?"

"No. It's none of my business," Sam said.

"Right. Just because we're not part of some religious mumbo-jumbo group, we're weird, right?"

"I didn't say that," Sam argued.

"You didn't have to. It was all in the curl of your lip." Grace shook her head. "Hypocrite."

"I didn't mean that. You're putting words in my mouth. Or in the curl of my lip." Sam's heartbeat hiccupped. She really did like Grace and didn't want to offend or upset her. She hadn't meant to do that at all.

"Since we're not some holier-than-thou Christian types, you think we're weird, don't you?" Grace's voice rose above a whisper.

"No." Sam licked her lips. "I don't."

"Sure. You can't even admit it, but you're thinking it," Grace said.

"I just don't understand it is all," Sam answered.

"Girls, is there a problem?" Mrs. Christian asked.

Sam turned to face the front of the room and shook her head. "No, ma'am."

Mrs. Christian sat back down.

"I'm sorry. I didn't mean to imply anything," Sam whispered over her shoulder. "And I don't think you're weird."

Grace remained silent.

The minutes felt like hours until the bell rang. Sam jumped out of her seat and faced Grace. "I'm really sorry. I don't think you're weird and I didn't mean to make a face of any kind."

Grace hugged her books to her chest. "Most kids I'm friends with think my family's weird because we aren't Christians." She headed toward the hall.

Sam fell into step alongside her. "I can't speak for anybody else, but I just don't understand it is all."

"What don't you understand?" Grace asked. She stopped in the breezeway right outside their math room.

Sam's heart caught sideways in her throat. So many times, Ms. Martha had assured them that when the time comes for witnessing, the Holy Spirit would give them the words. *God, I need the words now.*

She took a deep breath. "I just don't understand how anyone can learn about Jesus and not believe in Him." She paused, studied Grace's face to see if she looked mad. She didn't, so Sam continued. "And He's always there for me. He loves me more than even my parents and always wants the best for me." She shrugged. "It's like having my best friend in my heart, all the time. So I just don't understand why anyone else wouldn't want that ... this."

Grace shook her head. "I just can't buy into a loving Father or anything. Look at all the evil in the world. All the bad things that keep happening ... even that bomb at the theater. If there's a God who wants what's best, why does stuff like this happen?"

The same questions Sam wrestled with. "I don't know, exactly. But I believe in God. I believe in His Son. And that bomb at the theater could've gone off. People could've been hurt or worse."

"But that's just it, Sam. Bombs *do* go off. Planes crash. People die in car crashes. Bad stuff happens all the time. Where's your God in all of that?"

"I don't have all the answers, Grace. I wish I did. But I do know that our time here is marked in years, but after here? Yeah, that's forever. I want to have eternal life, and the only way for me to have that is to know that Jesus is God's Son, He died for me, and I accept Him in my heart."

The bell rang.

"I still don't buy it, but thanks for not thinking I'm a freak for being different," Grace said as she took two steps toward her own class. "See you tomorrow."

Sam rushed into her math class and sat at her desk,

but her mind wasn't on the Algebra equations Ms. Norton wrote on the board. Her heart felt extremely heavy.

Had she failed at her first real-live witnessing situation?

"Ms. Norton?" the school secretary's voice over the intercom interrupted.

"Yes?" the math teacher answered.

"Can you send Sam Sanderson to the office, please?"

Ms. Norton glanced to Sam's seat. "For checkout?"

"No. To see Mrs. Trees."

Ms. Norton raised a single eyebrow. "She's on her way."

"Thank you."

Sam stood, her knees a little weak as she took the pass the teacher handed her and left. She made her way down the seventh grade ramp, the wind almost whistling as it pushed through the open way. She took the four concrete steps down to the office and opened the door.

What had she done now?

CHAPTER 12

CUTTING TO THE HEART

A h, yes. Sam, come in," Mrs. Trees answered the knock.

Sam didn't recognize the scowling woman sitting in one of the chairs facing the desk, but her heart plummeted to her toes as she recognized the man wearing the bulldog expression. "Hi, Dad," she whispered.

"Hi, pumpkin." Well, at least he didn't sound angry with her.

Not yet anyway.

"This is Jessica Townsend," Mrs. Trees gestured to the woman.

Sam took a moment to scrutinize the lady's appearance. Short, dark hair with highlights in the front framed the woman's face, but what struck Sam the most was her thick, dark eyebrows. Not exactly a uni-brow, because they didn't grow together, but they were just so *thick*. Her scowl seemed to have deepened in the minute since Sam had entered the office.

"So you're the young lady wreaking havoc in my life," Jessica Townsend said. Her voice was nothing like Sam had thought it would be — instead of high-pitched and nasal, it was more hoarse, like she'd gargled with pebbles or something.

Sam didn't know what to say, so she kept quiet. The bell to change classes rang but was muffled in Mrs. Trees' office.

"Nothing to say to my face? You seemed to have plenty to say about me in your blog," Jessica said.

"Watch the attitude, please," Dad interjected. His bulldog expression morphed into something deeper, even more serious. The lines in the corners of his eyes drew his forehead down.

"Did I step on toes, Detective?" No mistaking the woman's snarkiness. "You'll allow her to smear my name but expect me to be cordial to the brat? I think not."

Dad stood. "And I think this conversation is over."

"Are you going to arrest me, Detective?"

"Let's all just take a moment," Mrs. Trees said, clearly out of her element in how to control the situation.

"Ma'am," Dad addressed Mrs. Trees, "you called me here to discuss my daughter's news articles and her reporting for the school paper. I didn't realize this was actually a confrontation. Had I known Ms. Townsend would be here, I wouldn't have come. She is a person of interest in an ongoing investigation that I'm leading. It's inappropriate for her to even be here on campus if she doesn't have a child enrolled in this school and inappropriate for you to have called me here under false pretenses, and," Dad glared at Jessica, "it's most certainly inappropriate for her to refer to my daughter as a brat."

Yea! Go, Dad. Sam caught her bottom lip between her teeth.

"Can't take the truth about your kid, Detective?"

"Ms. Townsend, please," Mrs. Trees said. "Mr. Sanderson, I'm very sorry."

Dad nodded, then grabbed Sam's hand and led her out of the office. The last few kids rushed to their third periods. The breezeway sat silent.

"You've stirred up quite the hornet's nest with your articles on that one, Sam." Dad shook his head. "She's one piece of work."

"They pulled the first article I had about her."

"Apparently not fast enough that she didn't see it. She told your principal she demanded to find out who told you about her childhood past when she hit a nun."

One of the security guards brushed past them on his way into the office.

Dad pulled Sam over toward the red brick wall. "Please tell me that she wasn't in elementary school when she lashed out at a nun who happened to be her teacher and you made it sound like she was an adult."

"Her childhood? Puhleeze. Dad, she was twenty-two when she hit that nun, who was not her teacher, by the way. She was living in a convent, supposedly planning on being a nun, but I don't know that for sure, which is why I didn't put it in my article. Anyway, if it was such a non-event like she's playing, there wouldn't have been charges filed and a court-ordered stay at the mental ward."

Ms. Townsend was definitely a piece of work. And to have the nerve to show up at a junior high school and demand to confront a kid ...

Well, Sam was more than a little unnerved by that. Seriously? A grown woman feeling the need to challenge a kid—what was up with that?

The bulldog expression returned to cover Dad's face. "How do you know all these details, Sam?"

"The court records of her case are a matter of public record, Dad."

His eyes narrowed down into little, bitty slits. "Yes, but you haven't been to the courthouse to read the transcript, and I haven't seen a huge bill on the credit card, so I'm pretty certain you didn't order a copy."

Her throat tightened. "Dad ..."

"This isn't a cloak-and-dagger game, Sam. This is very serious." He pointed toward the office. "That woman in there isn't playing. She's aggressive and antagonistic and has you in her sights."

"I know, Dad." Sam had to force the words past her ever-tightening throat to get them out. "But it's a matter of public record, so there's no *source* to name except public record. It's all in the court transcripts, right?"

"True enough. Okay. Listen, you go back to class. If you see that Jessica Townsend woman, you hightail it in the opposite direction. Do you understand me?" He crossed his arms over his chest. "I mean it, Sam. No trying to get a statement or anything for the paper. You go in the opposite direction. Don't even speak to her. Got it?"

"Sure, Dad."

He wasn't buying it. "No, not *sure, Dad*. I mean it, Sam. If I find out you so much as said hello to her, I'll ground you."

Ground her? For doing her job as a journalist? He had to be kidding.

One look at his face confirmed he wasn't. Not even a little bit.

"Okay, Dad. I won't."

He stared at her for a moment, then nodded. "Okay." He leaned over and kissed the top of her head. "Go ahead and go back to class. Mrs. Willis will pick you up this afternoon."

"Bye." She headed toward the media center for her third period class, computer keyboarding, then remembered she needed to grab her notebook from her locker. She turned the corner, out of sight.

"Oh, Detective."

Sam stopped as Jessica Townsend's voice called out to Dad. Sam inched down the wall and peeked around the corner.

"What do you want, Ms. Townsend?" Dad faced the woman as she approached him.

She stopped about two feet in front of him. "You'd be wise to warn your daughter of the dangers that come along with being a news reporter."

"Is that a threat?"

Sam's heart raced as she pressed closer to the wall so as not to been seen. She'd never seen Dad look like that. Mad, but in a calm way. It was really scary.

"Of course not. I would never threaten someone in the presence of an officer of the law."

"At least that's one smart thing you've said." Dad turned and headed down the stairs to the parking lot.

"One more thing, Detective," Jessica called out.

He stopped and pivoted. "What?"

"Before you haul me in for questioning, I had nothing to do with that bomb in the theater, nor did my chapter of the coalition."

Dad smiled. It was one of those smiles Sam recognized — the one Mom called his Cheshire Cat grin. She didn't know what exactly that meant, but she knew when Dad smiled like that, his sarcasm was likely to make an appearance. "I didn't ask you."

"But your daughter planted the idea, so you might. I'd hate to have to contact my lawyer and suggest you might be harassing me. Putting your daughter up to writing ugly things about me and all."

Putting her up to writing … Sam gritted her teeth. For all she knew, Dad didn't even think about Jessica Townsend being linked to the bomb.

Dad flashed that grin again. "You call your lawyer, Ms. Townsend. Matter of fact, maybe you should put him on speed dial. I have a feeling you might want a lawyer present real soon."

"Samantha Sanderson, what are you doing out here?"

Sam jumped and turned around. Heat burned her face from the inside out. "Oh, Ms. Pape. You scared me."

"What are you doing out of class?"

"Uh … Mrs. Trees called me. I mean, I was in her office. Now I'm going to class." It felt like her tongue was twisted into knots all of a sudden.

"So why are you standing out here?"

"I forgot my notebook. I'm going to get it."

"Then hurry up and do that."

"Yes, ma'am." Sam rushed to her locker. She got her notebook, then headed to the media center. She took her seat next to Makayla while Mrs. Forge droned on about not looking at your hands to type. It amused Sam to no end that keyboarding was mandatory, yet Makayla could run circles around most of the faculty. Especially Mrs. Forge.

"Where have you been?" Makayla whispered.

"Office," Sam whispered back, then filled Makayla

in on what had happened, and what she'd overheard between Jessica and her dad.

"Wow. That woman sounds like a freak," Makayla said.

Sam nodded. "She's a few colors short from a box of crayons, that's for sure."

"Doesn't it scare you? I mean, just a little? She pretty much threatened you." Makayla's big eyes went even wider. There might not be much Makayla couldn't do on a computer, but she didn't want to get in trouble.

But she did have a point. Not that Sam would ever admit to being scared.

"Dad put her in her place quick enough." Sam grinned at the memory. "That was really cool."

Makayla nodded. "I bet it was. I wouldn't want to cross your dad if he was mad."

Mrs. Forge gave them their assignments, then shuffled back to her desk. It wasn't a secret to anyone that she played solitaire all the time, but the kids loved it. Keyboarding was almost like having another study hall. As long as they didn't get too loud, Mrs. Forge concentrated on her game, only looking up when she won.

"So what did Mrs. Trees say about your articles? Was she going to take them down?" Makayla asked.

Sam hadn't really thought about that. "She didn't say." Surely she wouldn't take down today's post. But Ms. Pape had been on her way to the office ...

"Let's see." Makayla glanced to where Mrs. Forge sat behind her desk, her eyes glued to her screen. Mac's fingers flew over the keyboard. Within seconds, she was past the school's firewall and on the web.

"Look." She tapped the monitor, the paper's blog page loaded on the screen. "Your story's still posted."

Relief washed over Sam in waves.

"Oh. My. Gummybears! You have over four hundred comments." Makayla scrolled the mouse up and down to see the comments.

Four hundred? Sam leaned closer to the monitor. "Slow down, I want to read them."

Makayla laughed and let go of the mouse. "You go ahead and read them. I'm going to use your station to do the classwork."

Sam barely paid attention as she swapped places with her best friend. Her eyes drank in the comments as fast as she could read them. Most of them were asking for more details about Jessica Townsend hitting a nun or not knowing what the Central Arkansas Coalition of Reason was.

She skimmed through three hundred or so comments until she came across one posted ten minutes ago. From Jessica Townsend. Sam's stomach twisted as she read:

> I went to this school today to try and get an answer as to why I'm being slandered without cause, but this "Sam Sanderson" had her detective father show up and bully me before he stormed out. That's right, Sam Sanderson's father is the detective heading up this case. Appears

to me that he's using his daughter's paper to lead the investigation down the wrong path. Or is he asking her to report on things to distract everyone from the truth???

Sam felt like she was going to throw up. This was just what her father didn't need—what he'd probably been afraid would happen with her staying on this story. Maybe she should've done as he asked and let Aubrey give the assignment to someone else. Her dream wasn't worth hurting her father.

Lord, what do I do now?

CHAPTER 13

TO WRITE A WRONG

D ad?" Sam called out as she stepped from the kitchen. He'd come home, dropped his keys in the wooden bowl in the entry, then headed to his room just like always. But that was fifteen minutes ago. It never took him this long to lock up his gun.

She moved slowly toward the hallway. "Daddy?"

"I'm here." He shut his bedroom door behind him and gave her a quick hug. "Dinner about ready?" He led the way to the kitchen.

He might force a lighter tone into his voice, but Sam could hear the stress. Even if she couldn't, there was no way she could miss the deepness of the lines in his face which hadn't been quite so visible this morning.

"Yeah, I just took the casserole out of the oven."

"Good. I'm hungry." He cut the casserole and placed pieces of the chicken cacciatore on the two plates beside the helpings of sweet peas.

Sam set the rolls on the table, then put glasses of milk on the placemats before sitting across the table from him.

"It looks and smells great. Thank you. Do you want to offer grace over the food tonight?" he asked.

"Sure." Odd, because Dad always said the blessing. She closed her eyes. "Father, thank you for this meal before us. Please use it to nourish our bodies, and our bodies to honor You. In Jesus' name we pray and give thanks, Amen."

"Amen. Thank you. " Dad shoved a forkful of peas into his mouth and chewed with vigor.

She set down her fork. "Dad, what's wrong?"

"Nothing. Just hungry, like I said." He took a bite of casserole this time, still chewing almost in double time.

She stabbed peas off her own plate. If he wanted to be über polite like this, fine. Just fine. She chewed without tasting.

For the next several minutes, the only sound in the kitchen was of silverware scraping against glass and the gulping of milk. Even Chewy lay on the rug by the door, her head resting on her paws as she stared at her owners as if to ask what was going on.

As if Sam had any more clue than her dog.

Ten more minutes and Sam couldn't take any more

of the silent treatment or false pleasantries. "Dad, did you see the comment Jessica Townsend left on my post on the paper's blog?"

He wiped his mouth with his napkin, then slowly wadded it up and set it on his empty plate. "I did."

She waited …

Five seconds.

Ten seconds.

Thirty.

"And?" she asked. "What did you think?"

"I think Ms. Townsend still suffers from some mental issues." He ran a finger along the edge of his plate. "That is off the record."

The back of her neck went hot. "I know that."

"Good." He took his plate to the sink, threw away the napkin, rinsed his plate, fork, and glass, and then put them in the dishwasher.

Sam followed, doing the same, while he covered the other part of the casserole and put it in the refrigerator.

He wiped the counter without a word.

"That's it? That's all you have to say about it?" Sam crossed her arms over her chest and dug her hip into the side of the kitchen island. "No new warnings for me not to contact her? No telling me I should resign this assignment? Nothing?"

She was sick of his silence. She'd even risk getting in trouble by deliberately provoking him. At least he'd be talking.

Dad tossed the rag into the sink and stood across from her, almost mimicking her stance as he leaned against the counter housing the sink. "What do you want me to say, Sam? To stay away from her? I already told you that. That she's a few screws loose? You already know that. That I want you to give up the story? You already know that."

He ran a hand over his face. "But I don't really want you to give up the story. And your mom would certainly have my head if I tried to make you." He gave her a weak grin.

At least he was trying.

She crossed the space between them and gave him a hug. "I'm sorry if I'm making it harder for you to do your job. I'm trying really hard not to even ask you anything. I mean, officially."

"I know that, and I appreciate it." He hugged her tight, then kissed the top of her head. "Don't you worry about me. I'm fine."

She kept her arms around his waist and stared up at him. "Are you sure? If this is a problem for your job, I'll let Aubrey assign another reporter." She nearly choked on the words, but it was the right thing to do.

He smiled and squeezed her. "I thank you for the offer, because I know how much this means to you, but you don't have to do that, Sam." He let her go and folded the dishtowel on the counter. "Now, you go get started on your homework."

"Okay." She headed to her room. Dad still had something he wasn't telling her, but that was all right. Maybe he just had a lot on his mind with the case.

She opened her laptop and checked her email. Nothing of any importance. She checked the blog. Only a few new comments. Most of those were asking for clarification from Jessica Townsend's comment.

Lead the investigation down the wrong path, huh? *Well, we'll just see about that.*

Sam popped her knuckles just as her cell phone rang. She checked the caller-ID and grabbed it. "Hi, Mom."

"Hi, there, my girl. How's your day been?" Mom's voice always made Sam feel all warm and mushy.

The words tumbled over each other as Sam spilled the events of her day until she was done and out of breath.

"Oh. My."

"Dad didn't tell you?" It was one thing for him to keep something from *her*, but to keep something from Mom—that was serious.

"I haven't talked to him yet tonight." Mom's voice got all husky. "How did he seem at dinner?"

Sam told her.

"Well … if he doesn't want to tell you what's bugging him right now, nothing will get him to open up."

"True. But I am worried about him."

"I know." The smile came through in Mom's voice. "Now, what else is happening with you? Not about the story."

"Well …" Sam glanced around her room. She caught sight of her pom-poms on the dresser, safely out of Chewy's reach. "Our first game is tomorrow night."

"I hate to miss it."

"It's okay, Mom." Sam hadn't really given too much thought to cheering this week. Her mind had been wrapped totally around the bomb and suspects and articles.

What if she messed up in one of the routines? The rest of the squad would be furious with her.

And rightly so.

"I'll ask Dad to video some for me and then we can watch it together." Mom paused for a moment. "Are you nervous?"

"A little." Only because she hadn't practiced outside of her time with the squad.

"You haven't been concentrating on cheering much, have you?"

Sam squirmed. That guilty feeling returned. With a vengeance. "I've been busy, Mom. You know how time-consuming journalism can be." What, could Mom read her mind too?

"Oh, that I do. But you have to make sure you don't overextend your obligations."

"I know," Sam mumbled.

"It's hard to balance everything you want to do and everything you're good at, but sometimes you have to choose. You don't want to do things and not be able to give 100 percent. When you accept a position — cheer-leader, reporter, whatever — you accept responsibility for that. You don't want to let anything fall between the cracks."

Sam swallowed.

"I'm not getting on you, Sam. I'm just telling you to consider how you manage your time and responsibili-ties is all. I know how difficult it can be."

"I know, Mom." She did. It was just that she loved cheering but loved reporting too. Why couldn't she do it all?

"You don't want your grades to slip."

"Of course not. I'm studying just as hard, Mom. I promise." She'd worked hard to maintain her honor-roll GPA. *And* she took all pre-AP classes. Those advanced placement subjects were really tough sometimes, too.

"I know you are. Dad and I have always been very proud of you too. I just want you to know that it's okay if you feel overwhelmed and like you need to give something up. No one expects you to be able to do everything."

But she loved everything she was involved in. "Thanks, Mom, but I think I can manage."

"I just wanted you to know that Dad and I will sup-port you if you need to back out of something."

"Okay, Mom."

"What else is new?" Thank goodness she changed the subject.

Grace Brannon's image slammed into the front of Sam's mind. "Mom, do you have any friends who aren't Christians?"

"Uh, I guess I might. I don't rightly know. Why?"

"I do. I mean, I thought she was a Christian but she told me she wasn't."

"How do you feel about that?"

That was the question, because Sam didn't really know how she felt. "I guess I'm confused. I know God loves us and that Jesus died for us and accepting Him is the way to eternal life ..."

"But?" Mom asked.

"Well ... Grace asked me, If God is so good and loves us so much, then why do bad things happen to innocent people."

"What did you tell her?"

"Just what I know to be true: that I want to have eternal life after I die and the only way for me to have that is to know Jesus is God's Son, that He died for me, and I accept Him in my heart."

"You told her right." Mom's voice cracked a little. "It's hard to witness. It's hard to share your faith with someone, but you were honest and shared your feelings. That's all you can do, Sam."

But was it enough? "I don't know, Mom. She didn't seem changed by what I told her." Wasn't that the whole point of witnessing — to lead people to Jesus?

"Oh, my sweet, sweet girl. It's not for you to change

someone's heart. You're only to plant the seed by sharing your faith. God will do the rest."

"Yeah, I guess."

"I *know*. I'm very proud of you, Samantha." Unlike Dad, who only used her full name when he was mad, Mom used it when she was really, really emotional. Like now.

"Thanks, Mom. I love you."

Mom cleared her throat. "Okay. I've got to run or I won't get my article edited and sent in. I'll call you tomorrow night and see how your first game went. I love you bunches."

"Goodnight." Sam set down her phone and returned to the blinking cursor.

Jessica Townsend.

Maybe she shouldn't lash out and slam her like she'd intended. Wouldn't she be expecting that? Maybe, just maybe, she should consider taking a different path.

She grabbed her iPhone and called Makayla, who answered on the second ring. "Hello."

"Hey. Can you talk?" Sam asked.

"For a few. Mom's helping Chloe with her homework. What's up?"

"About Jessica Townsend."

"What about her?" Mac asked.

"Did you get the name of the convent she was in?"

"Hang on."

Sam stared at her pom-poms while she waited. She

wouldn't let the squad down. As soon as she finished the article and the one worksheet she had for homework, she'd practice the routines and cheers until they were perfect. The squad had practiced the stunts and pyramids during practice after school, so Sam felt pretty confident in those areas.

"Got it. She was in the Discalced Carmelite Nuns of Little Rock."

Sam jotted it down. "Here in town, huh?"

"Yeah. Part of Carmel of St. Teresa of Jesus on West 32nd Street. They're cloistered."

"What does that mean?"

"Um, kinda shut off from society, I think," Makayla said. "Oh, and they're a practicing discalced order, too."

Sam wrinkled her face. "What does *that* mean?"

Makayla laughed. "I had to look that one up. It means they either go barefoot or wear sandals."

"Why?" Seemed like a silly thing to announce they did.

"I'm not real sure. Had something to do with Francis of Assisi or Clare of Assisi. I don't know."

"That's weird," Sam said. What was the religious importance of going barefoot or wearing sandals, other than the fact that Jesus wore them? Then again, washing the feet was kinda big back in Jesus's time.

"I know, right?" Makayla laughed again. "Did you see Jessica's comments on your blog post?"

"I did. I'm working on my article for tomorrow right now."

"Ruh-roh, Scooby … guess this means you're writing about her again."

"I am, but not in the way you think."

"How's that?" Makayla asked.

It was Sam's turn to chuckle. "Well, I'm not 100 percent sure yet, but it won't be the flaming that everyone will expect."

"Interesting." There was a slight pause before Makayla whispered into the phone, "Oops, Mom's coming down the hall. See you in the morning."

Sam set the phone down and popped her knuckles again.

Interesting indeed.

CHAPTER 14

FOR THE LOVE OF THE GAME

… Jessica Townsend, the woman who heads up the local chapter of the Central Arkansas Coalition of Reason, an anti-God organization, spent over five years with the Carmelite Nuns of St. Teresa of Jesus, a convent so extreme they are cloistered *and* are so devoted to the order that they only go barefoot or wear sandals.

What do YOU think? Could someone who spent five years in a convent, practicing to be a nun, be capable of losing her faith? Or, do you think it's more likely that she only became involved in an anti-religious organization because of some other, personal and private reason? Sound Off, Senators. Leave a comment with your thoughts. ~ Sam Sanderson, reporting

"I totally don't see how this relates to the bomb,

Samantha." Aubrey crossed her arms and stared at her from behind her desk—the editor's desk.

Sam wanted to be in that chair next year. She licked her lips, swallowing back the sarcastic reply nearly burning her tongue. "It's a follow-up to yesterday's story."

"But that's just it — this isn't a story that has anything to do with the bomb."

Ms. Pape nodded. "I have to agree with Aubrey on this one, Sam."

The smirk returned to Aubrey's face. "We need something about the bomb, Samantha. Not rehashing of personalities of possible suspects."

"Mrs. Trees told me about the personal attacks Jessica Townsend made against you and your father yesterday," Ms. Pape said. "And I read her comment on yesterday's post. I must commend you for not lashing out and being ugly in today's, but the news about the bomb is getting a little lost."

"I thought your dad was going to give you information," Aubrey said.

"He can't give me inside information, Aubrey," Sam said. Yeah, she'd kind of implied he would back when she asked for the story initially, but whatever.

"No, but you can get information the same time it's released to other press outlets, right?" Aubrey asked.

"Uh, right," Sam said. Where was Aubrey going with this?

Aubrey's sarcastic look was cemented with her

smirk. "Then how come the front page of this morning's paper had information regarding the type of bomb and an idea of where it originated and you turned in nothing about the bomb itself?"

What? "Uh …"

"They got the report that the bomb was made using specifications found on multiple sights on the Internet, made with items easily purchased statewide that wouldn't raise any type of suspicion," Aubrey said.

At least it was only a report of a dead-end lead. Had there been a new direction, they'd probably be having a totally different conversation entirely right now. Sam didn't want to think about that.

"I understand how it can be tempting to want to be an investigative-type reporter, the one who gets to *solve* the case," Ms. Pape said. "However, a good reporter stays on top of the facts being released by law enforcement in order to have enough information to actually investigate." She smiled kindly at Sam, a complete opposite of Aubrey's expression. "Understand?"

Sam nodded. "Got it. I'll bring it more into focus for tomorrow's story."

"If it's not, I'll assign someone else to continue coverage," Aubrey said. "It might be a good idea to cut down the articles on this story anyway. I don't want it to seem that we're forcing a local news story just to move outside of the school for news."

"Good point, Aubrey," Ms. Pape said.

"I'll make sure I have a focused story tomorrow, with newsworthy information." Sam couldn't believe Dad hadn't given her the heads up about the bomb information. She'd have to make sure to cover it, but not just a repeat of what everyone else already reported. Something she could scoop the others with.

If this story went down, she'd be relegated back to interviewing teachers for study tips. Social suicide in the highest form. And forget having a chance at editor next year.

She returned to her area between Lana and Celeste.

"What did the she-beast want?" Lana asked.

Sam brought them up to speed on Aubrey's decision. "So I have to figure out something to write about that is directly related to the bomb." She sighed and leaned back in the chair. "I guess I'm going to have to steer clear of potential suspects."

"So, what are you going to write about?" Celeste asked.

"I haven't a clue." Sam stared blankly into space. What to write about? What? Something directly related to the bomb itself. No suspects. No —

"Sam!" the sharp voice blended with the fingers snapping in front of her face snagged her out of her thoughts.

"What?"

Luke Jensen stood in front of her, grinning. "You were really out of it, there."

Words failed her. She nodded dumbly as heat raced up her spine to the back of her neck.

"I just wanted to let you know that I think Aubrey's wrong. I think you're on the right track with the suspects."

Why wouldn't her tongue untie? Because Luke's dimples were just so cute. She nodded again.

Luke tilted his head and raised one eyebrow. "Well, okay. Good luck." He sauntered over and joined Kevin Haynes and the other guys.

Lana shoved her. "What is wrong with you?"

"What?" Sam asked. Her face felt like it was on fire.

Lana groaned and rolled her eyes. "You have a crush on Luke … he's over here trying to talk to you, and you're like some rabid mute person. What's up with that?"

"I was just lost in my thoughts is all."

"Yeah, sure, right. Happens all the time. Not," Lana said.

"Whatever," Sam said, her face hotter than hot. *Time to change the subject.* "I'm trying to figure out how to write about the bomb that doesn't shed any light on suspects and isn't just a repeat of what was in today's paper."

"Why don't you just ask your dad for an update?" Celeste asked.

She would read what the state's paper had to say, then try to get Dad to give her at least one little piece of new information. She had a game to cheer at tonight, so she wouldn't be able to do much hard research. He owed her for not telling her about the bomb anyway. The least he could do is help her out now.

"Did you hear about Nikki Cole's parents?" Celeste whispered.

"That they're divorcing? Yeah." Sam glanced across the newspaper room to Nikki, who sat beside Aubrey. Although Aubrey talked constantly, Nikki looked distracted. Sam couldn't even imagine how she'd feel if her mom and dad split up. "I feel really sorry for her."

"She looks sad," Lana said.

"Wouldn't you be?" Celeste asked.

Lana shrugged. "It has its advantages."

"Your parents are divorced?" The question slipped out before Sam could stop it. "I'm sorry, that was insensitive of me."

Lana smiled. "It's okay. They divorced last year. That's the reason I transferred to Robinson. Mom and I moved here to be closer to my grandparents."

"I'm sorry," Celeste said, with blush creeping over her face.

"Don't be. It's much better than having to listen to them argue all the time. Now, well, they both went through some sad times, but they aren't arguing anymore."

Sam swallowed hard. What kind of friend was she to not even remember Lana's parents were divorced?

"So you live with your mom?" Celeste asked.

Lana nodded. "For a while we stayed with Grammy and Gramps, but only for a few months until we got our own apartment."

"That's right—you live in those nice apartments right down from here," Sam said.

"Yep. It's kinda nice being just me and Mom. We each have our own room and our own bathroom."

"But don't you miss your dad?" Sam clamped her hand over her mouth. When was she going to learn to just shut up? "I'm sorry."

Lana smiled. "It's okay. And yeah, sometimes I really do miss my dad. But after his twin brother died, he started acting mad all the time. I don't know. I do miss him."

Despite Dad being strict a lot, Sam would miss him something awful if he and Mom got divorced.

"But a lot of kids don't get to see both their parents every day," Lana said. "Like military families. Some kids don't get to see their dad or mom in the military for months on end. I get to see my dad every other weekend at least."

"True," said Celeste, but she didn't look convinced.

"Or like Sam. Her mom is off on assignments a lot, so she doesn't get to see her every day."

She had a point. "That's right." But Sam didn't think that was the same. Her mom lived at the house with her and Dad. All of Mom's stuff was in the house, surrounding Sam and her dad. It wasn't like she was ... gone.

"With my parents divorced, Mom and Dad are almost in a competition to make sure I'm happy. So that means having the food I like in the houses, I get to watch the television shows I want, and I get to have friends over if I want." Lana shrugged. "Mostly, I'm just relieved to not have to listen to the fighting, then Dad slamming the door and roaring off in his truck, then Mom sitting in her room crying, and me pretending I can't hear her."

Wow. Sam really didn't know what to say now.

Lana cleared her throat. "It's all okay now." She stared across the room at Nikki. "But it takes a while to get used to the change," she almost whispered.

Yeah, Nikki was Aubrey's best friend, but somehow, Sam didn't think Aubrey was the compassionate type. Not like Makayla was there for Sam.

Did Nikki have anybody she could talk to?

"Gooooo Senators!" Sam and the other cheerleaders finished the cheer and, in unison, executed toe touches.

The crowd clapped and cheered as the football players returned to the field to play the last quarter of the game. The Senators trailed by six: thirteen to seven.

Sam smiled and waved at the micro video camera Dad held. It wasn't the same as having Mom here, but at least they'd be able to laugh over the video together later. Was that how it was for Lana?

She was still upset with Dad, but having practice after school until the game, she hadn't had a chance to talk with him. Once she did, though … she'd get a hit for something to put in Monday's article. Something everyone else didn't already have.

She turned to the side, locking her hands behind her back like they were supposed to. A kid walked by with his hands full of nachos. Sam wrinkled her nose as the smell reached her. Nachos were just plain gross. And they stunk.

Remy, the head cheerleader, called the next cheer.

As Mrs. Holt had taught them, Sam looked over the crowd's head, focusing on the press box at the top of the bleachers. The sun had just begun to set and cast strange shadows over the band and the rest of the fans. They looked like fingers reaching out to grab the people from their seats in the stands. Kinda freaky.

Kevin Haynes threw the ball. Luke Jensen caught it. Luke was usually second string but had been put in the game because the starting wide receiver was recovering from a strained ankle.

"Go! Go!" several men in the stands yelled.

Luke passed the thirty yard mark.

"Go! Go! Go!" Remy began the chant.

Luke spun out of a tackle and hit the twenty yard mark.

"Go! Go!" People in the stands stood.

The ten.

"Go!"

Luke dodged a final tackle.

"Go! Go!"

Luke crossed into the end zone. The crowd went

wild. The band started the school's new fight song. Sam and the rest of the cheerleaders launched into their dance routine for the song. She nervously counted it out in her head … five, six, seven, eight.

"Sing loud our victory song, our team is on the way." Right arm up, left arm up, right kick, left kick.

" … for we will win today, FIGHT, FIGHT, FIGHT." Round-over, stomp right foot, stomp left foot, shake poms.

Sam moved in perfect unison with the girls on either side of her. Right-ball-change. Left-ball-change. " … our opponents are now on the run."

Turn. "Hail, hail, the gang's all here." Kick. Kick. Shake poms. "And Senators will win tonight." Turn, wiggle. Jump around. "Fight!"

The crowd erupted with applause. As Sam tossed her pom-poms onto the ground in front of her, she caught movement in one of the finger-shadows from the corner of her eye. She narrowed her eyes and focused on the person standing at the bottom of the bleachers, their face half-masked from view.

The crowd stood and stomped as the game announcer came over the speakers — the extra point was good.

The figure turned as the crowd rose to its feet. Slowly … slowly … slowly …

Until he shifted to get around a kid running down the stands. Then Sam made eye-contact and gasped.

Frank Hughes.

CHAPTER 15

MUM'S THE WORD

"A re you sure it was him?" Dad asked for the millionth time as they headed to the school's parking lot.

Sam nodded. "I'm positive. What was Frank Hughes doing here, Dad?"

"It *is* a public event, Sam." He led the way to the truck. People whooped and hollered across the parking lot, celebrating the team's winning the first game of the season.

"But he doesn't have any reason to be here. And the theater's open tonight."

"Just because the business he owns is open doesn't mean he has to be present. There's such a thing as time off, you know." Dad clicked the button on his keychain and the truck's doors unlocked with a click. "You don't know that he doesn't have reason to be here. You shouldn't jump to conclusions. You know better."

"I do know." Sam tossed her pom-poms and megaphone into the backseat, then settled into the front seat and secured her seatbelt. "His daughter died in an auto accident a couple of years ago. She was his only child."

Dad started the car and waited for the opposing team's bus to clear the lane. "How do you know about that?"

Sam sighed. "I do my research, Dad." Well, Makayla had done it, but she was one of Sam's sources, right?

"His daughter, Trish, was seventeen. She was only out of drug rehab for a few months when she ran a red light and hit a car. Trish and the driver of the other car were both killed instantly," Sam said. "Unconfirmed reports said she had drugs in her system at the time of the accident." She glanced out the window as Dad turned the air conditioner on high.

Even though the sun had long since slipped below the tree line, it had to still be in the eighties. Maybe even nineties.

Dad shot her a quick look before turning the car onto Cantrell. "Where did you hear about the alleged drugs in her system?"

She sighed again. "Dad, you know I can't reveal my sources."

"Well, good thing you didn't put *that* in your article. Never, ever put something into print that you can't back up with more than *an unnamed source*. It's pretty much understood in the legal realm that the reporters who use that line are usually the ones making stuff up."

"Kinda like when cops say *no comment,* it's pretty much understood that they can't answer the question because they'll get in trouble?" she asked.

He chuckled as he turned onto Chenal Valley. "Yeah, something like that."

"You have to give people the benefit of the doubt, Sam. You can't let your over-active suspicious mind run away with you."

Her suspicious mind was just fine, thanks very much. "If he had a good reason to be there, why was he hiding in the shadows?"

Dad laughed aloud as he turned into their driveway and pushed the button. The garage door opened slowly. "Sam, half the bleachers are in the shadows for the first half of the game and it gets progressively worse as the sun sets." He pulled into the garage and turned off the car's engine. "You have to stop reading into every little thing."

Sam got her cheer equipment and headed into the house, not saying anything else. Dad assuming she was making a big deal out of nothing really burned. Seriously? Maybe Frank Hughes was the person who planted the bomb, and when she ran articles about his franchise and stuff, he got mad. Maybe he came to the game to get an idea of her routine. Maybe he would come by late tonight and watch her in her house. He could break in while they were sleeping, put a gag over her mouth —

Chewy jumped up on her, scratching her thighs under the hem of her cheerleading skirt. "Ouch, girl." Time to get the dog's nails trimmed.

Sam went to the kitchen door and let Chewy out. The dog immediately went off barking after a squirrel. Chewy stood woofing at the bottom of a tree, looking up, like she was surprised the squirrel had gotten away. Sam laughed. At least with Chewy around, Hughes couldn't sneak up on her.

Dad grabbed two water bottles from the fridge and tossed one to her. "You did really good tonight. All the practice is really paying off."

She twisted off the cap of her bottle. She had something she needed to say, and no point in delaying it any longer. "Dad, why didn't you give me the information about the bomb when it was released to other press contacts?" She struggled with keeping her voice even, knowing that if she raised her voice, she'd get grounded, and she really wanted to go to Playtime Pizza with Makayla tomorrow. They'd been looking forward to it.

"You didn't ask." He took another long sip of water.

What? "Dad, you knew I was the reporter covering the story. You could've just told me."

"I could have, but that wouldn't be you doing your job. That would be me doing it for you."

"Dad!"

"No, Sam. I don't call up all the other reporters every time we get a new piece of the case we can reveal. They call our press office at least twice a day, asking for updates."

"But I'm your daughter."

"Which is why you need to do it yourself. So you *can* claim your successes as your own and know I didn't give you any special favors."

His reasoning sounded right, but ... he was her *dad*. Didn't that count for anything?

He finished off his water and tossed his bottle in the recycling bin. "I don't want you to think I'm being unnaturally hard on you. I talked with your mom about this and she agrees it's the best way for you to learn to be a great reporter." He leaned over and kissed her head. "It's been a long, busy day. Why don't you hit the shower?"

After a shower, Sam *did* feel much better. It was amazing what ten minutes of hot water and some of Mom's Moroccan oil-infused shampoo could do. Though it still bugged her that not only did Dad not volunteer the information about the bomb, but Mom had agreed with him. She kind of felt like they'd betrayed her.

Once she braided her wet hair, she checked her email. Nothing new. She sent Makayla an email about the game tonight and seeing Frank Hughes. At least her bestie wouldn't think she was overreacting at seeing him at the game.

Too bad Makayla's mom thought football was too

dangerous — her word, not Sam's — so she wouldn't let Mac go to any of the games. It made no sense to Sam, since Mrs. Ansley had no problem with Makayla taking karate. Maybe it was just team sports she had a problem with. Poor Mr. Ansley ... Mac said her mom wouldn't even let her dad watch sports on TV if the girls were home.

Sam's dad would never think of making that rule. And neither would her mom. It was kind of a family thing to watch football. Well, at least one game a year. Mom always cheered for Louisiana State University and Dad rooted for the University of Arkansas, so they always watched when those two teams played each other. Sam cheered for both, which was a lot of fun since her team always won.

At least Sam would get to hang with Makayla for a long time tomorrow.

Sam's cell phone rang. She checked the caller-ID, then answered. "Hey, Lana, what's up?"

"I'm sorry to call this late, but I knew you'd still be up because of the game." Lana spoke very fast, not at all like usual.

"It's okay. What's wrong?"

"I'm at Chenal 9. I met Lissi, Ava Kate, and some other friends for the six ten movie. Dad was supposed to pick me up no later than nine, but he's not here. All the others have gone. I've called Mom, but she's not answering at the apartment or her cell. I tried calling my dad, but it goes straight to voice mail. I don't know what else to do. I thought since your dad's a cop and all ..."

"Are you there by yourself?" Sam asked as her bare feet thumped against the wood floor of the hallway.

"Well, there are people here, but nobody I know." Lana's voice dropped. "I'm in the bathroom. The kids coming in now are all older. High school and college age even."

"Hang on." Sam pressed the mute button. "Dad?" she called out.

"In here," he answered from the kitchen.

She found him putting together a sandwich. "The hot dog at the game didn't do it for me," he said, grinning.

"Dad, Lana's stranded at the movies and scared." She quickly told him about Lana's dad not showing up. "What should she do?" she asked as she opened the kitchen door and let Chewy back inside.

He put the plate in the refrigerator. "Tell her to go to the front, on the backside of the ticket counter. We'll go get her, but tell her to keep trying her mom and dad."

Sam pressed the button on her phone. "Lana, we're coming to get you." She told her what Dad had said while she went to her room to throw on some clothes.

"Thanks, Sam. I didn't know who else to call," said Lana. "Please hurry. I'm a little freaked out," she whispered into the phone.

"We're on our way." Sam hung up the phone, then

slipped on some clothes. *God, please be with Lana and help her not be so scared.* Sam met Dad in the living room. He looked so big and strong and … safe. "Thanks, Dad."

"No problem, pumpkin. Let's go."

Once out of the subdivision, Dad cleared his throat. "Did Lana get ahold of either of her parents?"

Sam shook her head. "I told her to text or call me if she heard from either of them."

"Do you know where she lives?"

"In the apartments right down from the school. She and her mom live there alone."

Dad nodded, but kept his eyes focused on the road.

"Her mom and dad are divorced."

Again, Dad said nothing.

Sam checked her phone. No text. No call.

Good thing the theater was close. Sam called Lana, who answered immediately. "Hello?"

"Did you get in touch with your mom or dad?"

"No. I've left messages for them both," Lana said. "I'm getting more than a little worried."

"We're almost there. Are you by the backside of the ticket counter?"

"Yeah. The manager or something saw me and he asked me what I was doing. I told him, and he wanted to call the cops, but I told him your dad was one and was coming to get me. He seemed to act like he knew who your dad was."

"Good. We're almost there." Sam remembered the night manager from the night the bomb had been found. Definitely a woman. "What's the manager's name?"

"Frank."

Sam's heart hiccupped. "Frank? You mean Frank Hughes? The owner?" The man who'd been creeping around her football game?

"Yeah! That's why his name sounded familiar. Your article. Duh. I completely forgot," Lana said.

"We're almost there, Lana. Just hang tight. Bye." She hung up the phone and told her dad Lana's side of the call.

"First he shows up at the football game, and now he just happens to notice Lana hanging out by the back of a ticket counter so he goes to talk to her? On a Friday night? I don't think so." Sam shook her head. "There's something going on with him, Dad. I just know it."

"Sam, I'm going to tell you something, but you have to promise, and I mean *promise*, not to breathe a word of it to anyone."

She sat up straighter in her seat. "What?"

"I mean it, Samantha. This is serious. You can't even tell Makayla."

That was serious. "I won't."

A minute passed in silence.

"I'm only telling you this because I really don't think I have any other choice."

She held her breath.

Dad parked the car and turned off the engine. He shifted to look Sam in the eye. "Frank Hughes has been getting hassled and receiving threats."

"What?"

"He'd been getting some random hang-ups for a couple of weeks before we found the bomb. He didn't think anything about them and certainly didn't connect them to the bomb."

"But they're connected?" Sam asked.

"We aren't sure, but they might be. Remember I told you on Wednesday that we found out about the insurance on the theater?"

She nodded.

"When we were at his office interviewing him, he received a call and was told he would be ruined, one way or another."

Ohmygummybears! This was better than ... well, than anything.

"He got a similar call yesterday. And today. The one today implied the bomb was just a warning."

At least it explained Dad's defending his being at the game tonight. "Who is it? Do y'all have an idea?" Sam's heartbeat sped.

"We don't know. The caller never stays on the line long enough to get a trace and uses a device to disguise his voice."

Jessica Townsend's image floated across Sam's mind. "Or her voice?"

"Or hers." Dad gave a nod.

Or, it could be Frank Hughes' accomplice. It could all be a hoax to distract the police from his outrageous insurance policy he'd hoped to cash in on. "What makes you so sure the calls are legitimate?" she asked.

"We were there when he got them." Dad's expression was stern. Like set-in-cement stern.

"How convenient, wouldn't you say?"

"We have no reason to believe otherwise. But either way, we're treating this as our strongest lead." Dad opened the car door. "Remember, Sam, what I told you is off the record. You can't use what I've told you. Understood?"

She nodded and climbed out of the car. Yeah, she understood. Understood she needed to get the story herself. Even Mom had agreed with Dad on that point. She fell into step alongside her dad.

What good was it to know something and not be able to use it?

Then she remembered a movie she'd watched not too long ago about a news reporter. The reporter had uncovered something she needed to use, but couldn't use it unless she found another source.

Sam smiled to herself as she followed her dad into the theater. She might not be able to use what Dad told her, but if Mr. Frank Hughes talked to her ... well, that was fair game.

CHAPTER 16

MOVING AHEAD

I can't imagine what's going on, Mr. Sanderson," Lana said from inside the theater's office.

Mr. Hughes sat behind his desk, facing the loveseat Lana and Sam sat on.

Sam's dad sat in the chair closest to the desk. "And you've gotten no response from either your mom or your dad?"

Lana shook her head, big tears shining in her eyes.

Please don't cry. Sam could understand Lana being upset, but she hated crying. Something about crying just really grated against her heart. She took hold of her friend's hand and squeezed.

"Can you tell me what the arrangements were supposed to be after the movie?" Dad asked Lana.

"Dad was supposed to pick me up after school, but

Mom told him I was meeting my friends for a movie." Lana stared at the carpet on the office floor. "He wasn't really happy. He said that I should visit with my friends during the week and not infringe on his visitation time, but Mom told him it was what I wanted, not her." She lifted her head and stared at Sam's dad. "I guess he accepted that, because he was supposed to pick me up at nine."

Sam squeezed Lana's hand again. It was sad to think your dad forgot you, which, obviously, Lana's dad had.

"What about your mom? Do you know if she had plans for the evening?" Dad asked.

Lana shook her head. "I know she was planning on meeting a friend for dinner at Bravo after she dropped me off at the theater, but that's it."

"Do you know who she was meeting?"

"Mrs. Tonti, a teacher at Chenal Elementary."

Dad made a note in his notebook. "And you haven't heard from either of them since you got to the theater?"

Lana shook her head. "No, sir. When the movie was over, I looked for my dad and didn't see him. I texted him, then went to get a refill on my drink while I waited for him to answer me." She shrugged. "I figured he would probably not want to come inside, so I needed to be ready to run out to his truck as soon as he texted back."

"So you didn't hear anything back from him at all?"

She shook her head again. "Mom either." She sniffed.

Don't cry. Sam squeezed her hand.

Dad handed Lana a piece of paper and a pen. "Can you write down your address, your dad's, and both of their phone numbers for me, please?"

She did, then handed it back to him.

Taking the paper, Dad stood. "I'm going to make a few calls. I'll be right back." He left the office, shutting the door behind him.

"It's gonna be okay," Sam whispered to Lana. Anything to keep the waterworks at bay.

The theater owner smiled at them, despite probably not wanting to. Sam wondered if he was thinking about his daughter. How he wouldn't have the opportunity to forget to pick up Trish from the movies or other mundane parental stuff. And Sam suddenly felt overwhelmingly sorry for him.

"Mr. Hughes, how're you doing?" Sam asked.

He tilted his head. "What do you mean?"

"I mean, how are you doing? How's business? I noticed one of those new security cameras when I came in."

"Oh." He nodded. "Well, business is going slow, but I anticipate it'll pick back up as time continues to pass with no further incidents."

"That's good." She could tell he seemed a bit leery of her. She could understand. Kind of. "I'm sorry if my article really offended you. I didn't mean to imply you, personally, had anything to do with the bomb," Sam said.

He smiled. "I admit, at first I was quite upset with

you, but I realize you were just trying to sensationalize the reporting."

Well, not really. She'd been factual and just tried to make people think for themselves. But she'd let it go. "I didn't mean to make a bad situation worse for you."

"I appreciate that," he said.

How could she get him to talk about the threats without letting on that she already knew? She had to be very careful. "I really am sorry for what's happening to you, Mr. Hughes." That was the truth, especially after learning about his daughter.

"Thank you. I'm confident your father and the rest of the police department will be able to find out who set the bomb and is making the calls."

Yes! He brought up the calls. "Making the calls?" she asked, focusing on keeping her tone very neutral so as to not to raise flags in his mind.

"Yes. The one today, well, I think the officer said he could pick up some of the background noises. He said he hoped to be able to isolate the sounds to hopefully give the police an idea of location possibilities."

Lana started to say something, but Sam squeezed her hand. Tight.

"What, exactly, does the caller say?" Sam asked, then held her breath. He knew she was a reporter assigned to the story. He hadn't told her the conversation was off-record. That meant anything he told her was fair game.

And Lana was here to witness that Sam hadn't broken any rules to get the information.

"Like I told your father, just random warnings and threats like *I'm going to ruin you like my life was ruined* and *you'll pay for what was done.* Stuff like that."

This was exactly what she needed: details Dad hadn't told her. Using this, he'd know she got the information on her own. Wasn't that what he wanted?

"And you have no idea who it could be?" Sam asked. Did he have that many people who hated him? Surely he had to have some idea who was upset enough to want to see him pay for whatever he did wrong.

But Mr. Hughes shook his head. "I've tried to think of anyone I could have possibly offended, even in the smallest of ways, and can't think of anyone who your dad hasn't already checked out and cleared."

Interesting. "What do you think they meant about paying for what you did?" she asked.

"I don't know, but they said I'd pay for what was done. I have no clue what they're talking about, much less who it could be."

The door opened and Dad stepped back inside. Good thing he hadn't come back a few seconds sooner. He would be livid if he knew Sam was questioning Mr. Hughes, even though she was in her right to ask questions.

"I've sent an officer to your apartment, Lana, to check on your mom. They couldn't get an answer when they knocked, so they're waiting on the manager to come and open the door," he said.

"I have my own key," Lana said.

Dad shook his head. "No need. The manager was just getting dressed, then would unlock the door."

"Oh. Okay." This time it was Lana who squeezed Sam's hand.

"I also sent an officer to your dad's place. There's no answer at the door, and there's no vehicle in the driveway. Do you know what your dad drives?"

"A Ford F – 250. White. He just bought it a few months ago."

"This year's model?" Dad asked.

Lana shook her head. "Last year's. He bought it used."

"Okay, we'll check it out." Dad shot Mr. Hughes a look, then looked back at Lana. "But we don't want to leave you here, so I think it's best if you just come home with us until we can find your mom or dad."

"Okay." Lana stood and answered so quickly that Sam wondered if she seriously thought they'd leave her here.

Really?

Sam stood as well.

Dad extended his hand to Mr. Hughes. The two men shook hands. "Sam, why don't you and Lana go ahead and get in the truck?" Dad handed her the keys. "I just have something I need to tell Mr. Hughes before we leave."

Man, she really wanted to stay and hear what they

were going to discuss, but Dad's brows puckered up and she knew the bulldog look would come right behind it. "Okay." She took the keys and led Lana out of the office. No sense fighting a losing battle.

Besides, she already had enough to start a killer article that was sure to scoop everybody.

"I'm really worried about my parents," Lana interrupted Sam's thoughts.

"I know. It'll be okay," Sam said with false confidence as they headed toward the theater's front door. But the truth was that she didn't know if it would be okay. She couldn't be sure. *God, please let it be okay.*

The warm night air wrapped around them like the quilt her grandmother had made Sam, and it was just as suffocating. Or maybe it was the situation that was making it hard for Sam to take a deep breath. Lana sniffled beside her. Sam knew she needed to be strong for her friend. She pointed into the sky. "Look, there's the Big Dipper."

Lana tilted her head and looked up. "I don't see it."

Sam leaned in close to her and pointed. "See that bright star right there?"

"Yeah."

"That's part of the top; follow it down." Sam moved her finger along the imaginary lines connecting the stars.

"Oh. Now I see." Lana smiled. "I've never been able to find constellations."

"Well, now you have."

The parking lot was filled with cars but very few people. The last showings of the night had already started, and the people from the previous ones had already gone home. Aside from Sam and Lana, nobody moved about.

Sam grinned and pointed at her dad's truck. "Race you." She took off without waiting to hear Lana's reply.

Lana's longer legs soon pumped her to the lead, but she reached the truck only a foot or so ahead of Sam.

"You cheated. I wasn't ready," Lana panted.

Sam laughed. "But you won anyway." She pressed the button on her dad's key ring and the doors clicked open. She opened the back door. "Slide over."

Once inside the backseat, Sam leaned into the front seat and stuck the keys in the ignition. At least that way she wouldn't lose the keys before Dad needed them.

"What do you think happened to my mom and dad?" Lana asked.

"I don't know." Sam sat back down beside her friend. She didn't want to point out how odd it was that both of them were missing at the same time. Especially since they were divorced and all. "I've been praying everything's okay."

"Me, too," Lana whispered. "I'm scared." She leaned over and rested her head on Sam's shoulder.

In the silence of the dark car, Sam couldn't help but wonder about Grace Brannon. When she was scared or worried, what did she do? Where did she find something to make her feel better? Praying always made Sam feel better, even when things didn't go her way. If she didn't have prayer … well, Sam didn't know how she'd feel. Sad most of the time, probably. Sam didn't think she would want to live that way.

"Check out that guy," Lana said.

"What?"

Lana lifted her head and pointed to a car creeping along the driveway in front of the theater.

Sam stared. The car moved slower than slow, with the headlights turned off. Only the little yellow lights under the headlights were on. It was a red, older, four-door car. Sam thought it looked a lot like Mrs. Willis' car. She could barely make out the shadow of the driver from the glow of the dashboard lights, but it was obvious the driver was staring into the theater. Looking for something specific. Or some*one* specific.

"The guy doesn't even realize he doesn't have his lights on," Lana said. "Oh, here comes your dad."

Sam jerked her gaze to the side door of the theatre. Sure enough, Dad crossed the concrete to the stairs. As soon as he did, the driver of the car must've seen him, too, because the car gunned off toward Chenal. Sam noticed that as soon as it made the turn around the corner, the headlights came on. *So it was deliberate that they hadn't been on earlier.*

Dad opened the driver's door. "Sorry it took a little longer than I thought."

"Dad, did you see that car?" Sam asked.

"What car?"

"The one that raced off when you were coming down the stairs."

"Yeah. I hope you kids know that it's not cool to gun your engine for attention."

"Dad, I don't think they wanted attention." Sam told her dad about the headlights being turned off and the creepy-slow pace.

"It was probably somebody just here to pick someone up."

"This late after the movie's over and the next one isn't over for another hour or so?" Sam asked.

He shook his head. "Sam, your suspicious nature just runs way too rampant sometimes." He started the car, but before he could back out of the parking space, his cell rang. He grabbed it from his hip. "Detective Sanderson."

It always gave Sam a thrill to hear her dad use his *police voice*, as she and her mom had dubbed it years ago.

"I see." He glanced into the rearview mirror.

Sam caught his look at Lana. The call must be about Lana's parents. Or one of them.

"Yes, of course."

Now Lana looked at Sam's dad, too.

"I'll be there soon. Thanks." He set the phone in the car's console, then turned to face the girls in the backseat.

"That was about my mom or dad?" Lana asked. The fear snaked into her voice.

Sam slipped her arm around Lana's shoulders and held her tight.

"Both of them." He paused and drew in a breath, making brief eye contact with Sam before turning his attention back to Lana. "They've been in a car accident. They're okay, for the most part."

Lana gasped and covered her mouth with her hands.

Sam put her arm around her friend.

"They've got bumps and bruises, and from what the officer just told me, your mom needed a few stitches on her forehead, while your dad broke his ankle."

Lana made a muffled cry from behind her hand.

"They're okay, honey," he said. "I'm going to take you to the hospital to see them now, okay?"

"They're really gonna be all right?" Lana asked, tears rolling down her face.

Sam hugged Lana harder.

"The officer said that's what the doctor told him. Their phones were turned off once they got in the emergency room, so that's why they didn't answer your calls. Your mom bugged the nurse to call the theater to get a message to you, but I guess it never made it." He smiled and nodded at Sam. "Y'all buckle up and we'll head to the hospital."

Sam gave Lana a final hug, then sat back and put her seatbelt on. One question burned in her mind: How were both of Lana's parents in the same car accident?

CHAPTER 17

THINGS THAT GO BUMP IN THE DARK

"'m just glad her parents were okay. I bet Lana was relieved to see them for herself," Makayla said as they waited in line at the Playtime Pizza buffet. The rich smell of freshly baked pizza pulled them through the line. They'd been looking forward to this Saturday treat all week long. Playtime Pizza was one of the funnest places in Little Rock.

Sam tapped her fork against the deep orange plastic plate. "She was. But get this: guess why her parents were in the car wreck together in the first place."

"Oh, I didn't think about that." Makayla slid a piece of cheese pizza onto her plate. "Give me a second to think."

Sam put two pieces of pepperoni pizza on her plate

and followed Makayla down the buffet. She added some mac 'n cheese. "Give up?"

"No." Makayla laid out a neat little salad beside her piece of pizza. "They're going in together to buy Lana a really cool birthday present?"

"Nope." Sam headed to the drink station and drew herself a root beer. She waited for Makayla to get her water, then led the way to one of the tables in the front. But not too close to the center stage. She didn't want to get roped into doing one of the group dances with the guy dressed up in the pizza dude "Pete Za" costume. It was kind of a creepy outfit. Sam had never liked it. Gave her the willies.

"Then I don't know. Wait, don't tell me that Lana's going to move?" Makayla asked. She sat down and prayed over their food, then took a bite of salad.

"Nope. Give up yet?" Sam bit into the pizza and sighed as the warm cheese and tangy sauce blended into a moment of pure happiness for her.

"Fine. Tell me."

Sam wiped her mouth and grinned. "They were going to a marriage counselor."

Makayla's eyes widened as she hurried to swallow. "Her parents are getting back together?" She took a drink of her water.

"From what they said, they're going to try." Sam took another big bite of pizza.

"Wow. I bet Lana's happy."

Sam nodded. "She is, but trying not to get her hopes up too high. She said that they've broken up and gotten back together before, only for it not to work out."

"Well, we'll just have to pray that it works out for them this time." Makayla, the eternal optimist.

"Yep." Sam finished off her pizza and mac 'n cheese. She glanced over the tables and caught sight of Dad in the corner, his cell phone pressed to his ear. She turned back to Makayla. "Are you done yet?"

"Almost." She took another bite of pizza, chewed fast, then swallowed. "Why are you in such a hurry?"

"Just ready to play some laser tag is all." And she didn't want Dad to get called in to work. If he did, he'd either make them leave or have Mrs. Ansley come stay with them, which was okay, but she'd bring Makayla's little sister and tell Mac she had to take her sister around with them.

"Fine." Makayla took a last drink of her water before wiping her mouth and then standing. "Let's go."

Sam waved at her dad. Then she and Makayla headed up the stairs to check in for laser tag. Hopefully they wouldn't have to wait long for a game.

They were in luck: the attendant told them he had three spots left open for the next game, which started in five minutes. They handed their cards to be scanned, then took their slip of paper printout with their player name and which laser pack number they were assigned.

Sure enough, in about three minutes, the attendant called them into the entry room.

Everyone took in how they looked in the black light, some giggling nervously at the eerie designs of some of the shirts they wore. Sam's shoelaces glowed. That's one thing she loved about this laser tag game — that it was played in black light. You could kind of see people, but not really clearly, which made the game more fun. Sam considered herself on the expert level.

Sam glanced around the room as the laser tag worker gave instructions on how to put on the pack and fire the gun. Lots of parents with their kids were in this group. She grinned to herself in the dark … lots of easy targets. The little girl in pigtails with her mom would be first. Sam could tell they'd never played before. They'd be toast.

The two boys with their mom would be next. Their mom couldn't even keep up with them in the entry room, so there was no way she would manage in the laser tag room that was designed with corners, turns, ramps, fences, and all sorts of obstacles to hide or set up ambushes behind.

Sam nodded to four guys she recognized as regulars. They'd be tracking both her and Makayla, ready to take them both out. They were really good at setting up ambushes. She'd walked into many of them.

Finally the attendant let them into the pack room. She rushed to her pack station, twenty-eight, and put the harness on over her head. She settled the heavy piece in place and grabbed the attached gun. She pressed both triggers and activated herself into the game.

She grinned at Makayla. Their strategy was always the same: split up, then hunt each other, taking out as many other players and racking up as many points as possible on the way. Their ongoing score stood with Sam in the lead by twenty-two points. Makayla held up one finger, indicating it was her turn to enter first. Sam nodded. She would have to wait at least ten seconds before entering the room to track Mac.

The attendant opened the door, and Makayla slipped through with the first group of players. Sam held back, letting the parents and their little kids get inside. All the better to rack up her points.

A man brushed by her, holding his son's hand. "Excuse me," he said.

"It's okay." She smiled at the little boy of about six, then glanced at the man's face to record it for points purposes.

She froze as she made eye contact with none other than Bobby Milner, leader of the Arkansas Society of Freethinkers and the first bombing suspect she'd featured in her articles.

He smiled and nodded, and she let out the breath she hadn't even realized she'd been holding. He didn't know who she was. Whew. She'd seen his picture on the radio station website, but none of the school reporters' pictures were up on the blog. Mrs. Trees had said it was for their protection. Sam and the other kids had argued to get their pictures up, but Mrs. Trees had held firm.

Sam was glad for that right about now.

Bobby and his son crossed into the room. Sam was the last one through the door. She needed to find Makayla.

The room was nearly pitch black, but the little colored lights on the vests glowed. So did the chalk designs drawn on the walls and ramps. And the special camouflage material draped over separators and fences and barrels. And some of the cutouts in the separators.

Bobby and his son were just to the right behind the first separator. Sam knew because she could hear him, and she recognized his voice from the radio interview. Good place for them to hide because nobody came past this area.

"Let me show you how we did it in real life," he said to his son.

"Did you do this kind of stuff in the Marines?" his son asked.

Sam pressed against the opposite separator where they couldn't see her, but she could hear them.

"All the time," Bobby answered his son. "Stay close to me and I'll show you how it's done."

Bobby was in the Marines? Sam flattened herself

against the makeshift wall, waiting until they passed. She waited until they turned to the right and headed down the ramp toward the fence and barrel area.

One of the little kids she'd seen earlier ran out in front of her. Instinctively, she shot his vest. His lights flashed. Hit!

He stared down at his chest, then looked at her. He started crying.

Sheesh. She turned and took out his mom as she ran toward him. Sam kept going, lasering the other kid before squatting to move under the separator to the left.

Bobby shot his laser beam on one of the older girls who'd entered at the same time as Makayla. The girl laughed, but Bobby took out her boyfriend as soon as he rounded the corner. The boyfriend wasn't amused. He grabbed his girlfriend's hand and led her around the ramp.

Sam waited until Bobby moved on, then she took out the other girl.

"Three minutes," the voice warned over the speakers.

She turned and followed around the corner where Bobby and his son had gone, then moved down the ramp. She could make out the lights on Bobby's son's vest. Sam smiled as she recognized where they were. Bobby was about to get taken out because he was heading to one of the regular's favorite ambush setups.

Holding back, Sam heard footsteps. She turned, laser

on, locked in on the little girl with pigtails, and fired.
The girl's lights flashed. Sam shifted the laser beam on
the girl's mom and took her out, too. The mom smiled
and directed her daughter down the opposite ramp.

Not wanting to miss Bobby being ambushed, Sam
hurried. She crouched and moved slowly … quietly. She
made out Bobby's stealthy motions. He held a finger to
his lips as he looked at his son. His son nodded. Bobby
leaned over and whispered something to his son. Sam
was too far away to hear what.

"Two minutes to go," boomed from the speakers.

Bobby jumped up, gun at the ready, and shot over
the top of the separator. A reflection of vest lights
flashed on the wall.

He crouched again, peeked around the corner with
his gun. The red laser beam split the darkness. Another
reflection of vest lights flashed.

One of the regulars charged down the ramp. Bobby's
son turned, the gun loose in his hands. The guy raised
his gun and Bobby's son's vest lit up.

"One minute until game over," blasted through the
darkness.

Bobby slid to the ground, laying on his back, and
shot the guy charging them, then rolled right and took
out the last guy in the group.

"Dude, you're good," one of the regulars commented.

Bobby clapped the guy on his shoulder. "I have

real-life experience in this, kid. I had to be good or I'd be dead."

"Really? That's cool," the guy said.

"Not a whole lot is cool about shooting or bombing people, kid," Bobby said.

Sam gasped, then her vest vibrated and her lights flashed. She spun to see Makayla grinning at her. "Gotcha this time, sucker."

"Game over," sounded. "Please return your packs to their stations." The low lights came on.

Vests vibrated. Sam checked her gun's screen. Ranked eighteenth. Seriously? She hadn't slipped lower than fifth in a long, long time. She couldn't be bothered with that right now. She grabbed Makayla's hand and pulled her back, letting the others go before them into the pack room.

"Why are you acting crazy?" Makayla asked.

"Shh," Sam whispered. "See that guy right there? The one with the kid?" She pointed at Bobby.

Makayla looked where she'd pointed. "Yeah?"

"That's Bobby Milner."

"From your article Bobby Milner?"

Sam nodded. "It gets better."

The laser tag attendant waved at them.

Sam hurried and removed the vest. She put it back on the rack, than grabbed Makayla's hand and left. She saw Bobby lead his son down the hallway by the black light golf course. Sam all but pulled her best friend toward the corner on the opposite walkway where she could see Bobby's every step.

"Are you sure that's him?" Makayla asked.

"Positive. The radio station put his picture up on the site by the link for his interview. I remember thinking he was younger than I'd imagined."

Makayla's gaze followed Bobby as he led his son down the stairs on the opposite side of the building.

"I overheard him talking to his son, then some other guys," Sam said. "He was in the Marines."

Makayla frowned. "So ... he's a hero?"

"No. Yes. I don't know. That isn't important." Sam pulled Makayla around the post so she could keep Bobby in her line of vision.

"Then what is?"

"I overheard him talking to the guys and he said he used to shoot and *bomb* people." Sam's heart raced just as it had when she'd heard him say it.

"He said that?" Makayla looked down at Bobby, who was pulling his son onstage to do one of those silly group dances with the costumed Pete Za.

Sam nodded as she watched Bobby make a horrible attempt at the chicken dance. Hard to believe that man down there who couldn't move to the beat was a Marine who shot and bombed people. "He said that. Those were his exact words ... bombing people."

Makayla didn't say anything.

"If he's trained to make a bomb, that makes him a top suspect."

"I wonder if your dad knows," Makayla said.

"I'm sure he does." But Sam wouldn't say anything about this to Dad. He'd made it perfectly clear she needed to ask all the right questions and get the leads all by herself.

And that's just what she intended to do.

"Want to hear something interesting?" Makayla asked.

Sam grinned into the iPhone as she plopped across her bed. "You finally beat me at laser tag?" She'd had so much fun today but was a bit tired now that she was back at home.

"Ha ha." Makayla chuckled. "But I did win."

Sam laughed.

"Serious now. Remember you asked me to look more into Frank Hughes' daughter and the rumor that she had drugs in her system at the time of the car accident that killed her?"

Makayla had Sam's full attention now. She sat upright. "Yeah?"

"Well, her blood tests were inconclusive for drugs."

What? "I don't understand. Drugs were either in her system or they weren't." Sam stood and began pacing.

"Apparently it wasn't that simple. Some of the

medications she was on as part of her rehab treatment can and do cause false positives in some of the tests," Makayla said. "No charges were filed with the state."

"Oh." Interesting.

"Anyway, that's all I know. Want me to look up anything else?"

"No. Thanks, Mac," said Sam.

"You're welcome."

"I've gotta run. Thanks again." Sam's mind went into overdrive. Something about guilt kept slamming in her head.

What was it?

Guilty. Blame.

If Trish Hughes's accident killed the other driver, and Trish also died, then who was to blame?

Sam stopped pacing and went in search of Dad, finding him "watching" a football game on television. Watching with his eyes closed, a trick he said he'd mastered long ago. Sam just figured it was an excuse to nap. "Hey, Dad," she said as she plopped down on the end of the couch.

His eyes popped open and he sat up. "Yeah, pumpkin?"

"What happens if somebody causes a wreck but they die?"

Dad wiped his eyes and hid a yawn behind his hand. "What?"

"If someone breaks the law—say, runs a stop sign or

a red light—and they cause a really bad accident that kills someone else, but they die too, what happens? I mean, the person who is at fault is dead, so they can't get a ticket or be punished, right?"

"Right." He yawned again. "Usually, in a case like that, if the family of the victim so desires, they file a claim against the person's insurance company."

"Oh." *What good did that do?* "For why?"

"Why?" Dad shook his head, as if to clear his thoughts. "For money."

"Money?" she asked.

"Yeah. They file a wrongful death claim, or whatever they call it. And the insurance company usually pays the maximum of the policy."

"What good is the money if their family member is dead?" Sam asked. It really didn't make a whole lot of sense to her.

"Well, sometimes their family member didn't die immediately. In that case, there are usually a lot of medical bills. And there are funeral expenses, which can be quite expensive." Dad frowned. "Why are you asking, Sam?"

She shook her head. "No reason, really. I was just curious." She jumped up from the couch and gave him a quick kiss on the cheek. "Thanks, Daddy." Sam rushed back to her room before he could ask her anything else.

Did whoever Trish Hughes killed in the accident have any family? Could they be behind everything?

CHAPTER 18

THE TRUTH, THE WHOLE TRUTH, AND NOTHING BUT THE TRUTH

Don't forget the youth rally next weekend. I expect every one of you to be there, ready to work," Ms. Martha said.

"Man, I'd forgotten all about the rally," Sam whispered to Makayla.

"That's why she reminded you," Makayla whispered back.

The youth rally was next weekend, and Sam was so excited. A whole weekend out at the Arkansas 4-H Center. Fun times with the youth group. They would canoe, swim, and play badminton, and in the evenings, they'd share testimonies and faith. It was always a special event.

Sam hung back a little after Ms. Martha released them to join their parents in the church's sanctuary.

"Come on. Mom will have my head if I'm not there to help her with Chloe before church starts," Makayla said. Mrs. Ansley sang in the choir, and it was Makayla's responsibility to watch her little sister during church.

But Sam's heart felt heavy. "You go ahead. I'll be right there. I just need to ask Ms. Martha something right quick."

Makayla raised her eyebrows but went on ahead. Fear of her mother's anger beat out curiosity.

Sam turned back to the youth room. "Ms. Martha?"

The youth director smiled. "What can I do for you, Sam?"

"I have a question."

Ms. Martha leaned against the desk. "Sounds serious."

Sam hopped up on the desk across from Ms. Martha's. "I have a friend who I just found out isn't a Christian."

"Ahh."

Sam waited, but Ms. Martha just stared at her.

"So, I, um ... well ..."

Ms. Martha smiled. "What's bugging you, Sam?"

"I told her about my faith. Why I believe like I do, but she doesn't seem to care." Yeah, Mom said it wasn't her job to change Grace's mind about God, but Sam just felt so … well, guilty. She had eternal life and knew it, but Grace didn't.

"You know, Sam," Ms. Martha began, "Sometimes changes in the heart start long before you see any outward changes in the person. When did you share your faith with your friend?"

"This week."

Ms. Martha smiled. "Then the gospel you shared is probably working its way from her head where she heard it, down into her heart."

"But she's heard about God before. She just doesn't believe." And it really worried Sam. What if something happened to Grace?

"You can't *make* someone believe, Sam. Faith can't be forced."

"I don't understand that." How would she reach Grace? Just sharing wasn't enough.

"Let me put it this way. You know how your mom and dad might love asparagus and eat it a lot, but you don't like it?" Ms. Martha asked.

Sam wrinkled her nose. "Asparagus is gross."

Ms. Martha grinned. "So your parents love it and eat it a lot and want you to try it."

"They're always telling me I should keep trying it. As if one day, out of the blue, I'm going to love it."

"Right. And they'll tell you it's good for you, that it has amazing nutritional value: lots of zinc, B6, vitamin C, K, phosphorus, and copper."

"Gross is still gross."

Ms. Martha nodded. "You trust your parents, right?"

Sam nodded, but she still wasn't going to eat asparagus.

"So your parents tell you asparagus is good for you, and you trust your parents, but you still don't like the asparagus."

"Right. It's gross, no matter if they try to hide it under melted cheese or not."

"That's not the point." Ms. Martha grinned and shook her head. "Now, I offered you asparagus at the cookout, and you told me it was gross."

"It is. What is it with you people and the green stalks?"

"Stay with me, here, Sam. So you wouldn't take the asparagus from me either, but you trust me, don't you?" Ms. Martha laughed. "I'm going to assume you do or you wouldn't be here talking to me right now."

Sam grinned. "Well, if you keep trying to shove asparagus down my throat all the time..."

Ms. Martha snapped her fingers and pointed. "That's it."

"Huh?" Sam must have missed something.

"That's the point."

Ms. Martha wasn't making any sense. "What's the point?"

"We were just talking about your parents trying to make you eat asparagus, then I talked about offering you some, and you said you felt like we kept trying to shove asparagus down your throat."

Sam didn't get it. "I was teasing you, Ms. Martha."

"I know. Well, for the most part." She smiled. "But you certainly aren't willing to try any asparagus right now, are you?"

"Uh, no." Sam had no clue what Ms. Martha was talking about. If she'd been confused before, Sam was *really* confused now.

"But, let's just say, that Makayla was eating a snack and munching on something you didn't recognize, but she sure was enjoying her snack. She offered you a bite and you took some. It wasn't what you expected, but it wasn't too terribly bad. That's when Makayla told you it was dried asparagus."

"Oh, that's really gross. And Makayla wouldn't eat the stuff either."

"But let's say she did and you took a bite and it wasn't too terribly awful. So, now you've tried the asparagus and it's not deadly. You don't want to go out and order any, but you aren't going to gag the next time someone offers you some. And maybe, later down the road, you might actually try it again, cooked a different way."

Sam crinkled her nose. "I don't think so."

Ms. Martha laughed. "Just stay with me for a minute."

"Okay."

"Just like your parents offered you asparagus and I did and you refused, telling me you didn't want it crammed down your throat …" Ms. Martha pointed. "Maybe your friend doesn't want faith crammed down her throat. But then, what if just like you took a bite of a snack Makayla offered you, and that little bite of asparagus wasn't all bad, your friend took that little piece of faith and ingested it?"

"So maybe down the line, my friend will try a little more of faith, right?"

Ms. Martha nodded. "Maybe. There's no guarantee, Sam, just like there's no guarantee you'll ever grow to like asparagus. But restaurants won't stop putting it on the menu just because you don't like it, so you'll still have opportunity to try it in the future."

"And just because she hasn't accepted Jesus doesn't mean we should stop sharing our faith with her, right?"

"Right." Ms. Martha smiled. "Make sense?"

"Yes. Thanks. Maybe I can invite her to the youth rally."

"Of course, but don't get your feelings hurt if she says no the first time. Sometimes it's a process. Now you'd better hurry to church or your dad's going to come hunt you down. The services have already started."

Sam hopped down off the desk and hugged Ms. Martha. "Thanks."

"Anytime," Ms. Martha called after her.

Sam stopped at the door and turned around. "Ms. Martha?"

"Yeah?"

"Seriously, you have to lay off the asparagus." Sam smiled and headed down the hall. She turned the corner and heard voices coming from the ladies' Sunday school classroom.

"I heard the police gave her a lie detector test and she passed with flying colors," a lady's voice said.

Sam turned, hearing their voices come closer. There was nowhere to go. Panicking, she slipped into a closet. The smell of old hymn books and mustiness accosted her. She pinched her nose to avoid sneezing.

"Are you sure, Vanya?" No mistaking that voice. It belonged to Ms. Kirkpatrick.

"I'm positive. Why, our own church member, Charles Sanderson, is the one who oversaw the testing."

Sam pressed her lips together. Dad?

"Well, if Charles Sanderson says Jessica Townsend passed her lie detector test, then I believe him," Ms. Kirkpatrick said.

"That's what I've been trying to tell you," Ms. Vanya answered, her voice getting harder to hear as she moved away from the closet.

Dad gave Jessica Townsend a lie detector test? And he didn't tell Sam?

She waited ten more seconds before cracking open the closet door and peeking outside. No one was around. She dusted off her arms after shutting the door. She sneezed. And again. Great. Now her allergies were going to go haywire.

Sam went into the ladies' room and blew her nose and washed her hands, then rushed to the sanctuary. She ran into her dad, literally, in the entry.

"Where have you been? I was getting worried about you," he said as he reached out to steady her.

"I'm sorry, Dad. I was talking with Ms. Martha and time just got away." She straightened and headed into the main room. She quietly slipped into her regular pew. Dad sat beside her.

As the congregation stood to join the worship team in singing, Makayla turned and shot her a questioning look.

Sam mouthed the word "later" and kept singing. It'd be fun to explain the asparagus to Makayla.

After church was over, Makayla handed Chloe off to her dad, then returned to Sam. "Okay, so what took you so long? Your dad asked me where you were and I didn't know what to tell him." She frowned. "Tell me you weren't snooping around or eavesdropping."

Heat filled Sam's face so she could only imagine how deep her blush was.

"You were!" Makayla shook her head.

"Not the whole time. I really was talking to Ms. Martha."

"About what?"

"Asparagus." Sam chuckled at Mac's confused expression. "I'll explain in a minute, but on the way to the sanctuary, I did overhear Ms. Vanya and Ms. Kirkpatrick talking."

Makayla shook her head. "Those two again? You know how they like to talk."

"But they were right last time I heard them talking, and I have a feeling they're right this time too." Sam quickly told her what she'd overheard. "And Dad didn't even tell me."

Makayla didn't say anything, but she had *that* look: wide-eyed innocence mixed with stern librarian.

"What?"

"Well, he can't really tell you things like that, Sam. It might cost him his job."

"Like he didn't tell me about the bomb details but released the information to all the other press outlets." Sam shook her head. "His excuse then was that I hadn't asked. Like I knew the information would be available? No, Mac, he just doesn't want his captain's son, Doug York, to go whining to his daddy that I know more about the case than he does."

"I don't know ..." Makayla wore uneasiness as smooth as she wore her hairband.

"I do." She wouldn't tolerate Mac defending Dad. Not when he had all but told her she wasn't doing her job. Even worse, he'd told Mom. "So it's up to me to get information when and where I can."

"I think you ought to step away for a bit. You're upset and not thinking this through. You don't want to act now and then regret it later, after you can't do anything to fix it."

"Ha. There's always a retraction option," Sam teased.

But Makayla wasn't laughing. "You and I both know a retraction is not a joke."

"Ma-kay-la," Mrs. Ansley hollered out.

"Mark my words, if you spout off when you're upset, you'll regret it." Makayla wagged her finger in front of Sam. "Call or text me later, girl." She turned and ran to her car before her mother could call for her again.

Sam headed across the hot parking lot to meet Dad. It didn't matter how Makayla tried to justify why Dad withheld the information from her, the point was that he did. Knowing how important this was to her, and even after she offered to let the story go for his sake. Sam gritted her teeth. There was no excuse.

Dad already had the air conditioner on high as she climbed into the front seat and fastened her seatbelt. "That's twice in one day you've pulled a disappearing act on me." He grinned as he put the truck in drive. "Are you practicing to be a magician?"

She couldn't even smile at his lame joke. It also probably didn't help that she was more than a little upset with him.

"What do you want for lunch? We have Big Orange, Bravo, Chipotle … well, you know what all's in the area. What sounds good?"

"I don't care." She wasn't really hungry, to be perfectly honest.

"What's wrong? Are you not feeling well?" Dad asked as they stopped at the red light.

"Dad, did Jessica Townsend pass a lie detector test about being involved with the planting of the bomb?"

"Where did you hear that?" Dad's expression went as tight as the seatbelt across Sam's chest.

The car behind them honked.

"Dad, the light's turned green."

He went through the intersection, then whipped into the Walgreen's parking lot. Dad put the car in park but left the engine running. "Samantha, where did you hear about Jessica Townsend's lie detector test?"

"So it's true?" She had to admit, she was a little intimidated by Dad's intensity, but she needed to prove she was a real reporter. Had to prove it.

"Samantha!"

"She passed a lie detector test?"

He was not amused. "Samantha, I need to know who told you that."

She shook her head. "I can't reveal my sources."

"That's twice you've gotten information that hasn't been released. I need to know where you heard this. I'm not playing."

"I'm not either, Dad." She shifted in her seat as the car seemed to get hotter, and it had nothing to do with the temperature outside and everything to do with

Dad's mood. "You know that a good reporter never reveals her sources." Especially when the information was obtained through eavesdropping methods.

"Samantha, this is serious. Someone in my department is talking, and that's not allowed. This is how cases are lost." Dad's grip was so tight on the steering wheel that Sam could see the veins in his hands. Even under his tan.

But she couldn't give in, no matter what. Just like he had to be professional, so did she. "I can't, Dad."

"Even if I ground you?"

He couldn't be serious, could he? Grounding her for not ratting someone out? This had to be some sort of test or something. She took a deep breath. Even if he did ground her, she had to stick by the journalism rule. No one would ever trust her if she gave up a source.

She sat as straight as she could and crossed her arms over her chest. "Even then. I can't give up my sources."

CHAPTER 19

RULES AREN'T MEANT TO BE BROKEN

I can't believe he threatened to ground me." Sam paced her bedroom, pressing her iPhone close to her face. She'd been so angry, wanting to call her best friend and rant, that she hadn't even bothered to use her Bluetooth headset.

"Calm down. You're giving me a headache," Makayla said.

"Sorry." Sam took two more steps, then turned suddenly. She stepped on Chewy, who'd been trailing her since she got home. "Oh, sorry, Chewy." She bent down and scratched the dog's head.

"What did you do to that sweet puppy?"

"Nothing. Stepped on her. She was behind me and I didn't see her. Can you believe he threatened to ground me if I didn't give up my source?" She still couldn't believe him.

"But he didn't."

No, she wasn't going to let him off the hook. "But he *threatened* to, Mac. That's wrong on so many levels that I can't even begin to count the ways."

"I tried to warn you not to say anything when you were this upset."

"This upset? I'm this upset because he threatened to ground me for not telling who told me information for my article."

"Sam, no one told you the information. You were eavesdropping."

Why did Mac sound like an adult all of a sudden? It was really annoying. Seriously annoying.

"It doesn't matter. Reporters have sources and we're supposed to protect them. Think how it would be if word got out that I'd revealed a source to the police. I'd never get anyone to talk to me. They wouldn't trust me enough to talk to me."

"Listen to yourself. A source didn't talk to you in the first place."

"That is not the point."

"You would rather get grounded than tell your dad you heard about the lie detector test by eavesdropping?"

Sam let out a long, slow breath. Why was Makayla being so dense about this? "Mac, it doesn't matter if someone told me to my face, told someone else to tell me, left me a voice mail, emailed it to me, or if it was overheard — I still wouldn't tell."

"But don't you see? All those other examples you gave were about someone giving you the information. That isn't the case. Here, you took the information without permission."

Sam paced faster. "So, you're saying I stole the information?"

Chewy jumped on the bed and stared at Sam with big eyes.

Makayla didn't answer for so long that Sam started to wonder if the call had been dropped. But, no, she could still hear her breathing. "Mac?"

"Well, you kinda did, Sam." Her voice was very low, her tone soft.

And it made Sam even more mad. "I didn't steal information. I overheard something that wasn't confirmed, so I tried to get confirmation from a reliable source. He confirmed in a no-comment kind of manner." She turned and stomped even harder on her next pacing lap. "I am under no obligation to tell him how or where or who I get my information from. Period."

"You don't need to yell at me. It's rude when I'm just pointing out the truth."

"You accused me of stealing information. That's rude."

"There's no talking reason to you right now when you're so mad," Makayla said.

"You're right. Bye." Sam ended the call and tossed her phone onto her bed. "Uuuuh." She fisted her hands into balls. "I can't believe she took Dad's side." She turned and made another lap in her bedroom. "Stealing information," she mumbled. "I didn't steal anything."

Her cell phone rang. Probably Makayla calling back to apologize. Sam wasn't quite ready to get over it.

Ring-ring-ring!

Well, she couldn't expect Mac to understand the strict rules of journalism.

Sam snatched up the phone. "Hello."

"Hi, Sam. It's Lana."

"Hey, girl." Sam dropped to the bed and rolled onto her back, letting out a long breath. "What's up?"

"I just wanted to thank you and your dad again for the other night. I was really freaked out."

"No worries." Sam ran her fingers through Chewy's thick fur and wondered if Chewy got as hot as Sam's long hair made her.

"I think Mom and Dad might make it this time around in counseling."

"Yeah?"

"Yeah. This time they're seeing a counselor the church recommended."

"Oh, that's great, Lana."

"And Dad's getting some grief counseling for losing his twin brother. They think that might've been the start of some of his anger issues. We have our first family counseling session tonight."

Sam didn't even know what she should say, so she just shared what she felt. "I'll be praying for all of you."

"Thanks, Sam. You're a great friend."

"You'd do the same for me," Sam told Lana, but it was Makayla's smile she saw.

"Hey, I gotta go. Talk to you tomorrow. Bye."

Sam hung up the phone and rolled onto her back again. She wished Mac would call now. But the phone didn't ring. The ceiling fan went around and around and around.

Chewy plopped on Sam's pillow, then closed her eyes.

Sam shoved the dog softly, laughing. "Hey, it's not bedtime yet, lazybones. Let's go for a walk."

At the word *walk*, Chewy leapt off the bed and went to the door, tail wagging.

Sam shook her head and smiled. "Dog, I swear you understand English." She slipped on her flip-flops, shoved her phone in the pocket of her capris, grabbed Chewy's leash, then opened the bedroom door. Chewy raced down the hallway, her nails tapping on the wood floor. Yep, she needed to remember to trim the dog's nails when Mom got home.

Dad sat in his recliner, football on the television.

"I'm going to walk Chewy." It was kind of asking, right?

"Got your phone?" Dad asked, but his tone was sharp.

"Yes, sir."

"Be back before it gets dark." His eyes never left the television.

"Yes, sir." Sam snapped Chewy's leash on her collar, then opened the front door.

For a minute there, she wondered if Dad would tell her she couldn't walk the dog. Sounded crazy, but no crazier than threatening to ground her for not giving up her sources.

God, am I just being stubborn here?

She rounded the corner and headed down to the cul-de-sac one block over. Chewy tugged on the leash and Sam picked up the pace.

I don't want to be mad at Dad, God, because I know I shouldn't. But it just seems so unfair.

She thought about Frank Hughes's daughter … losing her seemed pretty unfair. She even thought about Jessica Townsend … having mental issues probably seemed unfair to her.

With every fast step she took, Sam's anger slipped a little further away. By the time she reached the cul-de-sac, she wasn't mad at all.

But she wouldn't tell Dad that Ms. Vanya had been

the one talking about the lie detector test either. She'd gotten over her anger, but she hadn't gone stupid.

She decided to walk the opposite direction than usual on the way back home. It was a longer route, but she felt bad that she hadn't taken Chewy on a real walk in a couple of days. Besides, the weatherman forecasted rain starting tomorrow and going through the better part of the week, so she needed to let Chewy get as much walking exercise as she could while the weather was nice.

Her pace slowed as she looked at the flowers blooming in people's carefully planted flowerbeds. Collegiate flags flew from porches. Honeybees buzzed past. The sweet smell of honeysuckle lingered in the hot breeze.

All the green plants made Sam think about asparagus. She smiled. She'd never be able to look at the vegetable the same again. Not that she could look at it before. No matter what comparisons Ms. Martha made, asparagus was gross. And it stunk.

She rounded a corner and a cat shot across the yard by the sidewalk. Chewy barked and bolted. Sam grabbed the leash with both hands and pulled. "No!" She planted her feet and jerked the leash harder. "Chewy, no!"

The leash went slack as Chewy returned back to the sidewalk and stared up at Sam with her big brown eyes, feigning innocence.

Sam couldn't resist. She knelt and hugged the dog.

Movement across the street caught her attention. If it was another cat . . .

Luckily it wasn't. Just a man getting into his car. Sam stood and started to walk, but he looked a little familiar. She looked again but couldn't see his face as he turned and got into the car. He backed it out of the driveway and into the street, paused, then put the car in drive. Sam got a good look at him then.

It was Frank Hughes.

How did she not know he lived so close?

A car inched up, one that had been parked on the street. Sam hadn't realized someone was in it until just now when it pulled up. Something about that car . . .

It was the same car she and Lana had seen at the movie theater. The older, red, four-door car.

Had someone been parked on the street, watching Mr. Hughes' house and waiting for him to leave? What were the odds of seeing the same car at both Mr. Hughes's place of business and now here at his home? No way was this a coincidence.

Sam pulled her iPhone out of her pocket and turned as the car passed her. An older woman drove. The woman didn't even glance in Sam's direction, her focus was so intent.

Sam snapped several pictures of the car and the license plate before the vehicle sped off in the same direction Mr. Hughes had gone.

Dad might still be upset with her, but considering

the case was his and Mr. Hughes had been getting threats, he wouldn't ignore this. He couldn't. At the very least he could run the license plate and see who owned the car. Sam could describe the woman.

She tugged the leash and began to jog toward home. Chewy ran to keep up. Once home, Sam took off Chewy's leash and they both ran to the kitchen to grab water.

Dad still sat in his recliner, looking as if he hadn't moved at all since she left.

"Dad?"

"Yeah?" He didn't even look at her.

"I saw Mr. Hughes."

That got his attention. He muted the game on TV. "Where?"

"Leaving his house. Well, I guess it was his house. I'm not sure. He was leaving a house on Calais Cove."

"At any rate, you saw him?"

Still so terse. Sam pulled up the pictures on her cell and passed the phone to her father. "Remember the other night at the theater when I told you I saw that car going by real slow with its headlights off? You said it was my suspicious imagination? Well, that's the car." She pointed to the picture on her phone.

Dad scrolled through the photos.

"It had been parked on the street and I didn't see anybody in it. Then Mr. Hughes leaves, and suddenly that car starts up and moves in behind Mr. Hughes. I recognized the car, so I snapped a couple of pictures." She crossed her arms over her chest and sat on the arm of the couch. "A woman was driving."

Dad used his fingers to blow up the image on the screen. "I'll call this in and run a check real quick." He grabbed his own cell from the table beside him. "Hey, this is Sanderson. Need you to run a plate for me." Dad listed off the numbers and letters, then handed her iPhone back to her. "Yeah. Thanks."

"It might be nothing, Sam." Dad's voice wasn't nearly as abrupt as before.

"But it might be something." She fought not to sound too excited. If he again thought this was just her "over-active imagination," she didn't know what she'd do.

Dad shook his head. "I can't tell you what I find out, Sam."

"But I saw the car ... I took the pictures!" He wouldn't even have this lead if it weren't for her!

"And I appreciate that and your reporting it, but I can't take a chance on unreliable information getting out."

Unreliable? "Dad, I *saw* the car there myself. Both times."

"I'm sorry, Sam."

But he didn't sound sorry. This was just punishment for her not telling him who her sources were.

So unfair.

Sam stomped to her room before she said

something that would definitely get her grounded. Why couldn't Mom be home? She understood but was … where was Mom this time? She should be here instead of out working on her own career.

No, that was unfair. Sam threw herself face down on the bed. She wasn't mad at Mom. It wasn't her fault.

Now Dad … he was a totally different story.

She rolled onto her back and hugged her pillow to her chest. What could she do? Dad wasn't going to give her any information, even though he wouldn't have the information if it wasn't for her.

Maybe she shouldn't even consider the red car's driver just yet. Maybe she should concentrate on the story. What she knew.

She sat up in bed and grabbed her iPad. Sitting with her legs crossed, she set a pillow in her lap, then typed in what she knew about the suspects.

1-Frank Hughes owns the theater and carries a lot of insurance on it. BUT he's getting threats. (Could he be faking the threats to throw suspicion off of himself? Or do these threats have something to do with the death of his daughter and the driver of the other car?)

2-Jessica Townsend has mental issues and attacked a nun and is a spokesperson for the Coalition of Reason. (She passed a lie detector test, supposedly.)

3-Bobby Milner was a Marine, shot people and used bombs, is a vocal anti-religious leader of the local atheists group. (But he's a dad and has a kid — would he risk

hurting a kid with a bomb? He is used to it. AND he did
have that domestic abuse charge.)

Sam popped her knuckles. She highlighted Jessica
Townsend. Yeah, she was off her rocker, but according
to Ms. Vanya, she'd passed a lie detector test that Dad
gave her. Even upset with him, Sam knew he was a great
detective.

She hesitated, then highlighted Frank Hughes. She
didn't understand all about the insurance, but Dad said
he'd been there when one of the threats came in. Sure,
Mr. Hughes could have an accomplice and that's how
one of the calls came when Dad was there, but Sam
didn't think so. Apparently Dad didn't think so either.

So that left Bobby Milner. He was, in Sam's opinion,
the likeliest suspect. Trained and familiar with bombs,
anti-religious, and he had an abuse record ... sure
sounded like a prime candidate for the guilty party.

But, a woman had been driving the red car. That
would exclude Bobby Milner. The woman hadn't been
Jessica Townsend either. So who was she?

Maybe that's who Sam should focus her attention
on. Who was the woman in the car? What was her
connection to Frank Hughes? And Sam couldn't forget
about the car accident. Was that the connection?

CHAPTER 20

MONDAY MADNESS

… What do YOU think? Who is the person who has threatened to ruin Frank Hughes like their life was ruined? Who told Mr. Hughes that the bomb in the theater was only the beginning? Does this person drive the Ford that was seen prowling about at both the theater and Mr. Hughes's home?

And what about Bobby Milner, ex-Marine who said himself he'd shot and bombed people? Sound Off, Senators. Leave a comment with your thoughts. ~ Sam Sanderson, reporting

"I can't believe you saw the same car that we did at the theater," Lana said. "That's super creepy."

"Yeah. I left out that it was a woman driving. I didn't want to tip my hand with all the information." Sam smiled as she accessed the newsroom's Internet link, even though little twinges of guilt threatened to steal the smile right off her face.

When Dad saw the article, he would go ballistic. But she hadn't used him as a source. At least, not exactly. She'd focused entirely on what Mr. Hughes had told her, using his statements as the basis for her article. And her own eyewitness accounts, of course.

Still, Dad would most likely be furious.

Well, served him right. Kind of. He should have told her who the red car was registered to, but he'd refused, even though he wouldn't have even had that lead without her. So she could almost dismiss her feelings of guilt.

Almost.

Sam went to the *Arkansas Democrat Gazette*'s website, then opened the search for obituaries.

"Whatever are you doing?" Celeste asked.

"Looking for Trish Hughes's obituary." She typed the name in the search box on the website.

Lana leaned in. "Why? You already know how she died."

"That's not what I'm looking for." Sam took note of the date of the obituary, then closed out that search and opened another. This time, she put the date of Trish's obituary in the search box.

"Then what are you looking for?" Lana asked.

The results loaded. "Hang on." She scrolled through the six obituaries.

First one was a woman of eighty-two who died from a long battle with cancer. The second obituary was a man who died in a nursing home. The third reported a man who died while serving in the military. The fourth obituary was about a man who died unexpectedly. The fifth was a woman who died in the hospital. And the sixth obituary was about a thirteen-year-old girl who drowned.

Sam shivered.

"What are you looking for?" Lana asked again.

Sam clicked the listing for the fourth obituary. "Him." She clicked on his name, bringing up his obituary.

Jimmy "Big Jim" Needles passed away unexpectedly on Friday. A retired Green Beret veteran, he is survived by his wife, Ella. He is preceded in death by his parents, Adam and Rachel, and his sister, Amy.

Sam checked the dates. That Friday was the date of the accident. She nodded. "That's him."

"Who?" Lana asked.

"What are you talking about?" Celeste asked.

"The man who was in the accident with Trish Hughes," Sam said. "He died instantly, just like Trish. His name was Jimmy Needles." She wrote his name on the notepad. "His wife is Ella Needles." She continued writing.

"I know her," Lana said.

"What?" Sam asked.

Lana pressed her lips together tightly.

"You know her? Ella Needles? How?" Sam asked.

"I don't know if I can say anything," Lana said.

Oh, not Lana too. Sam was sick and tired of everybody telling her they couldn't tell her something that she knew good and well was important to the case. "Lana!"

"Well, we aren't supposed to share stuff from counseling. The personal stuff." Lana shook her head. "I've probably already said too much."

"Wait a minute." Sam held up her hands as if to stop everything. She really needed her mind to stop racing so she could process.

Ella Needles was the survivor of the person Trish Hughes killed in the accident. Lana's family was going through counseling. That couldn't apply to Ella Needles.

Sam closed her eyes. What was she missing?

"I don't follow," Celeste said.

"Shh." Sam needed to think. Lana's dad had anger issues. He and Lana's mom were having couples therapy through their church. Her dad ... grief counseling.

That applied to Ella Needles.

Sam stared at Lana. "You met Ella Needles at a group counseling, something for grief counseling. Because your dad lost his twin brother and she lost her husband. That's it, isn't it? I'm right?"

Lana chewed her bottom lip. "I don't think I can say."

Sam swallowed the groan. "It doesn't matter. I know

I'm right." She stared back at the screen. Something wasn't right.

"I still don't understand," Celeste said.

"Wait a minute." Sam tapped the notepad. What was she missing? She glanced at the date of the obituary. That was it!

"Her husband died over two years ago, but Ella's still in counseling?" Sam asked no one in particular, not that she expected an answer. Did it usually take that long to work through grief? Sam didn't have any idea.

"Grief isn't the same for everyone," Lana said. "That's what the counselor told us anyway."

But two years ago?

If Ella Needles felt like she needed to exact revenge on the Hughes family, why wait two years? What happened?

Or, Sam thought with a sinking feeling, was she totally off base with her line of thinking?

No, she couldn't be. Because if she was wrong about this, she had nothing else besides Bobby Milner, and while he looked like a good suspect, Sam couldn't get the image out of her head of him doing the chicken dance at Playtime Pizza with his little boy.

The chicken dance. Really? Hard to imagine anyone who did the chicken dance, publicly, would plant a bomb in a movie theater. It just ... well, it just didn't *feel* right to Sam.

Wasn't Mom always telling her to trust her gut instincts?

Right now, her gut was telling her — quite loudly — that Bobby Milner wasn't really a viable suspect.

So that left Ella Needles.

"Ms. Pape?" the student worker's voice over the intercom interrupted all conversation in the newspaper classroom.

"Yes?" Ms. Pape answered.

"Could you please send Sam Sanderson to the office for checkout?"

"She's on her way." Ms. Pape waved at Sam.

Checkout? Immediately, Sam's heart caught. Had something happened to Mom? To Dad?

"I didn't know you were getting checked out. Are you going to miss cheerleading practice?" Celeste asked.

"I didn't know I was getting checked out. Let Mrs. Holt know if I don't show up for practice." Sam grabbed her backpack and slung it over her shoulder.

"Hey, call me if you need anything," Lana said.

"I will. Thanks," Sam said, but her legs moved fast toward the office, as if trying to keep up with her racing mind.

She turned the corner off the seventh grade ramp and went down the first set of stairs, then all but ran down the second set. Her hand shook as she reached for the door knob to the office.

"I was checked out?" Sam said.

Mrs. Darrington, the school secretary, looked up from her desk. "Sam, your father is with Mrs. Trees in her office."

This. Was. Not. Good.

Sam's feet dragged along as she made her way down the hallway to the principal's office. Every muscle in her body tensed, desperately wanting to turn around and run from the office. Fast. Very fast.

She knocked softly on Mrs. Trees' door.

"Come in," Mrs. Trees answered.

Sam pushed the door slightly open. "You wanted to see me?"

"Come in. Sit down." Mrs. Trees pointed to the empty chair beside Dad.

Dad wore the bulldog look … intensified to the twelfth power. Squared.

She flashed him a nervous smile and dropped into the chair.

"Samantha," Mrs. Trees began, and Sam knew right then that she was sunk. "Your father has come to me and requested that I remove you from your current *Senator Speak* assignment."

"Why?" She stared at him. Surely he still couldn't be mad about her not revealing her sources.

"We'll discuss this privately, Samantha. Mrs. Trees just wanted you to know that it wasn't her decision to remove you, but mine."

"But Dad — "

He stood. "That's enough. Be grateful your principal talked me into allowing you to remain on the newspaper staff at all. I was fully prepared to have your schedule changed." He nodded at Mrs. Trees. "Thank you."

Mrs. Trees stood and shook dad's hand over her desk. "Anytime, Mr. Sanderson." She threw Sam a look of pure sympathy. "I'll see you tomorrow, Sam."

Sam stood even though her legs felt too weak to support her.

"Let's go," Dad all but growled.

This was worse than she could have ever imagined. He was beyond mad. He was furious. Sam followed to the parking lot. She buckled the seatbelt without a word.

They rode home in silence.

Once home, Dad parked the car in the driveway, just outside the garage. He turned off the engine but didn't open his door. Sam didn't know whether to stay put or go inside and go to her room like she usually had to do when she got in trouble.

"I asked you to do one thing, Samantha. One. And you deliberately disobeyed me." His voice sounded steady but monotone.

It scared her a little. "What did I do?" She made sure to keep her own voice soft so it didn't sound like she was being defiant.

"I told you about Frank Hughes getting threats in confidence. You promised you wouldn't breathe a word of what I told you, not even to Makayla." He swallowed, his Adam's apple bobbing up and down. "So imagine my surprise when I read your article in today's school paper."

"But I didn't, Daddy." She hated the whining tone that slipped into her voice, but she couldn't help it.

He shook his head. "Samantha. You deliberately defied me. You wrote about the one thing I told you not to use."

"No, Daddy. Every single fact I used came straight from Mr. Hughes. I didn't put anything in the article that he himself didn't tell me."

He kept shaking his head. "I don't care how you try to reason this, Samantha, you took information I gave you in confidence, that I had your promise was off the record, and used it for your article."

"Dad — "

"That you used only Mr. Hughes' statements in the article isn't the point. It's that you used the information I'd given you off the record to ply statements from him." He took a slow breath. "You betrayed my trust." His voice caught on the last word.

Trust.

Her heart caught as tears burned her eyes. "Dad." Her own voice cracked.

"Just go inside, Samantha. We'll talk about this more when I get home." He held up his hand in surrender.

"Please, don't argue anymore. Just go on in. Do your homework." He pressed the garage door opener.

Blinking back the tears, she opened the car door, then rushed inside. Dad closed the garage door behind her.

Sam ran into the kitchen and couldn't hold back any longer. The sobs exploded from deep inside her. She sat on the kitchen floor, her back against the island, and her head buried in her arms resting on the top of her drawn-up knees.

Chewy rushed in and licked her face.

She reached for the dog and hugged her. Chewy's whole body shook as she continued to lick Sam's face.

At least somebody still loved her.

CHAPTER 21

BENCHED

Sam stared at the clock on her iPhone. She'd finished her little crying fest but still wanted to talk to somebody. Needed to talk.

She dialed her mom's number. Even if she woke Mom in the middle of the night, Mom wouldn't care. She'd talk to Sam and make her feel better. But the call went straight to Mom's voice mail. Sam hung up without leaving a message.

Staring at the time again, she considered her options. Too early for Makayla. School wouldn't be out for another fifteen minutes, and Mac's bus wouldn't get her home for another twenty minutes after dismissal.

It wasn't fair. Dad should've given her the chance to explain. He could've understood where she was coming from. It was like he didn't care. And ordering her to be removed from the assignment. That was low.

Aubrey would be thrilled. She'd probably already handed the assignment over to Kevin Haynes. Fresh tears pooled in her eyes. She brushed them away and opened the refrigerator. She didn't feel like picking out a casserole for dinner. She was pretty much sick of casseroles anyway. She didn't want anything to drink, either.

She didn't feel much like doing homework. Or watching television. She didn't even feel like eating some of the ice cream Mom kept hidden in the back of the freezer behind the ham. She really needed a hug.

She slammed the fridge door and stared out the window.

Mrs. Willis bent over her flower beds, her big floppy hat drooping over her face.

Sam moved closer to the window, watching her neighbor. Mrs. Willis carefully placed a delicate plant in the flowerbed, shook some plant food around, then gently pressed potting soil around the fragile stem. She would finish with one, move down about six inches, then start again. Slowly. Carefully. Despite the sweltering heat, she continued to work with precision and care.

Suddenly, Sam wanted to talk to Mrs. Willis like never before. She grabbed her cell phone and slipped it into her pocket, poured two glasses of lemonade, and then headed out the side door. She crossed the hedge fence between the two houses.

"Well, hello, Samantha, dear," Mrs. Willis said as she approached. "Why, is that lemonade?"

"Yes, ma'am." Sam handed one of the glasses to the older lady.

"Dear, you are an angel." Mrs. Willis took the glass and sat back on her heels before taking a long sip. "That's mighty good lemonade." She took another sip.

She must be thirsty because the lemonade was a mix, and not even one of the more popular brands. Sam just smiled and took a little sip of her own. "I thought you might need a little break. It's so hot out."

"It is that, dear." Mrs. Willis rocked herself to where she could pull up to standing. "Let's go sit on the swing in the shade and enjoy this lovely lemonade."

Sam joined her on the padded double swing under the big old oak tree. She leaned her head back as they settled into an easy rocking.

"So, you want to tell me about it?" Mrs. Willis asked.

Sam opened her eyes and squinted at her neighbor. "Tell you what?"

"Whatever it is that's bothering you." She took another sip of her lemonade. "I can tell, you know. It's all over your face that something's got you all worked up."

Sam traced the lip of the glass with her finger. "I upset Dad." Wasn't that an understatement? "Actually, I made him mad. Really, really mad." Madder than she'd ever seen him.

Mrs. Willis let out a little laugh. "Well, that does tend to happen between fathers and daughters, dear. It's part of the cycle of growing up."

"I don't know, Mrs. Willis. I didn't just make him mad. He said I betrayed his trust." Sam toed a rock on every backward push.

"Oh, my. That is a tough one. Betrayal of trust is always hard."

"But I didn't betray his trust." Not really. Well, not in the way he said she did. "And he wouldn't even let me explain."

"That's unusual for your father, isn't it? Charles has always impressed me as a fair man. A just man."

"Not this time. He punished me without even really listening to my side."

"He grounded you?" Mrs. Willis had one eyebrow raised. It made her glasses look crooked on her face.

"No, but he went to my school and told my principal to remove me from a newspaper assignment. Without even listening to a single thing I said." Sam could only imagine all the mean and ugly things Aubrey would say. What she'd tell everybody on the newspaper staff. What she'd tell Luke Jensen.

She swallowed the mountain that lodged in her throat. Talk about an epic failure. Sam couldn't even bear the thought of going to school tomorrow. Everyone would be talking about her and how her daddy pulled her off a story. It was humiliating.

"That is rough, indeed." Mrs. Willis took off her hat and wiped her forehead with the back of her hand. "I know how much you want to be a journalist, like your mother."

"Yes, ma'am."

Mrs. Willis said nothing, just took another sip of lemonade and fanned herself with her big ole' floppy hat.

Finally, Sam couldn't stand it. "So, what should I do?"

"What?" Mrs. Willis looked at her as if she'd just asked what the square root of infinity was.

"What should I do? To make Dad forgive me?"

"Land sakes, dear, I don't know."

An adult who didn't have the answers? "You can't give me any advice?"

"Advice I can give you, Sam." Mrs. Willis chuckled and took another sip of lemonade. "Let me ask you this: *Did* you betray your dad's trust?"

"I — "

Mrs. Willis held up a finger. "Wait a minute. Think about that question."

Sam shut her mouth.

"The word *betray* means 'to reveal or disclose in violation of confidence,' but it also means 'to disappoint the hopes or expectations of.' She put her hat back atop her head. "With those definitions in mind, did you betray your dad's trust?"

She didn't exactly reveal anything Dad had shared with her, but she probably did disappoint his expectations of her. At least, she was pretty sure she had. Sam kicked the rock harder. "I guess he might think that I did."

"Guess. Might." Mrs. Willis shook her head. "Pshew, dear, those are some weak possibilities, as my momma used to say."

That sick feeling on the edge of Sam's stomach dropped a little lower. "Yes. I can see how he might feel as if I betrayed his trust." Just saying the words made her tongue feel like she'd eaten something slimy and icky. Like asparagus. "But I didn't mean to."

"Well, if you hurt somebody that you didn't mean to hurt, what do you normally do?"

Sam gave her a funny look. "I tell them I'm sorry."

"Bingo!" Mrs. Willis pointed at her.

Sam shook her head. Mrs. Willis didn't understand. "I didn't hurt Dad's feelings. I made him mad. Super mad." It was hard to apologize to someone who was just angry. They usually didn't want to forgive you until they cooled off.

"Honey, anger is nothing more than an expression of hurt."

"No, he was angry, not hurt."

Now it was Mrs. Willis who shook her head. "Dear Samantha, I forget how young you are. Most certainly at the root of every ounce of anger is pain. Hurt feelings, physical hurt, even spiritual hurt. When people are hurting, they sometimes lash out in anger. That's an easier emotion to deal with than pain." She wagged her finger. "Don't you prefer anger over hurt? Don't you enjoy holding onto anger, feeling as if someone's done you wrong, than to admit how hurt you feel by what they did or said?"

Sam had never considered that before.

"Telling someone you're sorry when you really are goes a long way in healing a lot of hurt." Mrs. Willis patted her leg. "Now, I have to get back to my flowerbeds. Thank you so much for the lovely lemonade and the delightful conversation." She hefted herself off the swing.

Sam took the glass and stood as well. "Thank you, Mrs. Willis." She gave the kind lady a quick hug.

"You're quite welcome, my dear." Mrs. Willis headed back to her flowerbeds.

Sam returned home. After putting the glasses in the dishwasher, she took a casserole from the freezer, put it in the oven, and set the temperature. She headed up to her room to do her homework.

She glanced at the digital frame with the scrolling articles and pictures of Mom with her awards. Maybe Sam wasn't cut out to be a journalist after all.

No, she wouldn't think like that. Even though Dad had taken her out of the game, that didn't mean she couldn't continue to follow the leads. What kind of journalist would she be if she stopped just because things got rough for her? She needed to stick with it. Prove herself.

She lifted the lid on her MacBook and opened a fresh page in the search engine. She typed "Ella Needles" in the box, then hit enter.

The results loaded, and Sam scanned. She clicked on the link for *Arkansas Business*, then read the article that popped up on the screen about how Mrs. Ella Needles had lost her civil "wrongful death" suit against Mr. Hughes and his insurance company in regards to the death of her husband.

Sam stared at the date of the article: two months ago. Wasn't that about the time Dad said Mr. Hughes reported he started getting hang-ups? *This* was the trigger that set her off . . . she didn't just wait two years to start exacting her revenge — she'd been waiting on the outcome of her civil case. She'd lost two months ago and decided to take it upon herself to get even with Mr. Hughes.

Ohmygummybears! It all made sense. The "you'll pay for what was done" and the "I'm going to ruin your life like my life was ruined" made sense now. The wording had bugged Sam. It wasn't "you'll pay for what you did" but instead was "for what was done." In Mrs. Needles's instance, those phrases actually made sense. She probably drove an older year, red four-door, too.

Now that she knew, she had to do something. Tell someone.

Dad.

He was mad at her, but he'd have to listen. Especially

if she apologized like Mrs. Willis explained. Maybe he'd even be so happy his case was solved that he'd forgive her.

An hour later, Sam had just finished her homework when Chewy jumped off the bed, barking as usual. Dad must be home. Sam glanced at the clock. It'd taken her longer to do her math worksheet than she thought. Dad was a little late.

Man! The casserole. She'd forgotten to set the timer. She could only hope it wasn't burnt. Overcooked enchilada casserole was just gross.

She ran to the kitchen to check the oven. She turned it off and grabbed hot pads as Dad's keys landed in the wooden bowl with a clank.

Her heart sped up a little. Nerves. It was hard knowing you needed to apologize for something so big. She turned as footsteps echoed on the floor.

"Mom!" She tossed the hot pads onto the kitchen island and ran to her mother.

Mom's arms wrapped around her and drew her close. Sam inhaled, breathing in the spicy scent of Chanel's CoCo, Mom's signature perfume. She immediately felt better. About the struggles with the story. About losing the assignment. About everything.

"Oh, I missed you, my girl," Mom whispered as she took a step back and kissed Sam's cheek.

"Dad didn't tell me that you were coming home early." Sam hugged her mom again before releasing her.

"I just decided to come home early this morning after I spoke with your father."

Sam's happiness took a crashing dive. Dad called and told Mom what she'd done? And Mom had felt like she needed to come home early because of that? Sam didn't know what to say. She'd messed up big time.

Dad came into the kitchen. "We need to talk with you, Samantha." He leaned against the kitchen island.

She swallowed. Hard. Even though her mouth felt as if it was stuffed with a wad of cotton balls. "Dad, I understand, but there are a couple of things I need to tell you first." She blinked several times as tears threatened to return. "First off, I'm sorry. I didn't think I was betraying your trust when I wrote the story and only used Mr. Hughes' statements. I'm sorry I followed up on a lead you told me in confidence. I understand now that even though I didn't actually use the information you told me, I disappointed your expectations of me. I'm very sorry, Dad."

Mom moved beside Dad and slipped her arm around his waist.

Sam couldn't blink back the tears in her eyes, but she forced herself to continue. "I realize now I might have put you in a very bad position at work too, and I'm really sorry. I really am, Daddy. I love you and I hope you can one day forgive me." She sniffled, hating that she was standing and blubbering like a baby.

He took the steps to close the distance between

them and pulled her into his arms. "Pumpkin, even
when I'm mad at you, I always love you and I always
forgive you."

She squeezed him. Hard.

"I'm sorry too. My captain was breathing down my
neck about your articles, thinking I had passed along
confidential information to you. We later found out
that Vanya Grossman's nephew is a clerical worker in
our precinct. Apparently, he likes to talk about cases
to make people think he's more important than he is."
He kissed the top of her head before letting her go.
"It didn't take me long to figure out that you got your
information from Mrs. Grossman since we all know how
much she likes to ... um ... *share* information."

Mom gave her a quick hug. "Sam, sometimes you
have to weigh what you report. It's a fine balance to
decide what truths to publish." She ran her fingers
through Sam's hair. "I sometimes have to remind myself
of what Proverbs 22:11 tells us: 'One who loves a pure
heart and who speaks with grace will have the king for a
friend.'"

"I think Mom's trying to say that you have to judge
by what your pure heart tells you, and to always speak
with kindness," Dad said.

Mom grinned. "Yeah. What he said." She laughed
and winked at Sam. She moved to the counter and sat
on one of the barstools.

"I'm proud of you for apologizing, Sam. I know that

had to be hard for you when you must be disappointed that I had you removed from the story," Dad said, taking a seat on the stool beside Mom.

Ohmygummybears! She'd almost forgot! "Dad, I know who planted the bomb, and why."

He smiled. "We already have the culprit in custody."

Her bubble burst. She leaned against the opposite side of the island. "Ella Needles?"

Dad's brows shot up. "How'd you know it was her?"

She quickly told him everything. "So it *was* her?"

He nodded. "She was already on our radar because of losing the lawsuit, but you helped cinch the case for us."

She what? "How'd I do that?"

"It was her red car you saw at the theater and at Frank's house. She'd been trailing him, trying to get up the courage to hit him like his daughter had hit her husband."

"Oh, that's awful." And it was, but Sam couldn't help being excited that she'd not only been right but had also helped the police with their case.

"We picked her up this morning. Luckily, she didn't see your blog post and flee before we could bring her in."

Heat burned Sam's face.

"Once she was in custody, she confessed to everything." Dad rubbed at a water spot on the granite counter. "As a matter of fact, it seemed like she wanted to be able to tell someone. I think she needed to get it off her chest."

But a couple of things still bugged Sam. "Dad, how did she know how to build a bomb? And plant it?"

"Guess where she met her husband."

Sam shrugged.

Dad grinned. "They were in the military together. Both trained in explosives."

Wow. That was crazy. Then again, that's one of the reasons she'd considered Bobby Milner a suspect. Right concept, wrong person. "What about why she set it to go off when she did?"

"Well, according to her, after her husband was killed in the accident, her church family basically chastised her for filing a civil suit against Frank Hughes and his insurance company. She says they told her she should have let it go. She couldn't and said they'd turned on her."

Mom reached across the counter and patted her hand. "Some people let their grief twist them up so much that they lose sight of their faith."

Made sense, but how ... incredibly sad.

"Don't worry about her anymore, Sam. You have to trust that the justice system and God will take care of her," Mom said.

Despite the reassurances, Sam would worry, but she'd do the only thing she could — the best thing she could: she'd pray for Ella Needles, Frank Hughes, and even Jessica Townsend. Oh, and Grace Brannon. And Lana and her parents. And Nikki Cole and her parents.

Maybe she'd better write down her list.

CHAPTER 22

AND THEN THERE IS TOMORROW

I'm really sorry for being so rude to you, Mac." Sam hugged her friend the next morning in the cafeteria before school.

"Aw, you know I love you like a sister." Makayla's smile always brightened Sam's day.

Sam saw Grace Brannon walking to a table on the other side of the cafeteria. "I'll be right back," she told Makayla before racing over to Grace.

"Hey, Sam," Grace said.

"Hey. I wanted to invite you to come with me to our youth rally next weekend at the Arkansas 4-H Center. It's with my youth group at church. We go canoeing and swimming and play badminton. At night, we sit around the campfire and roast marshmallows and share what's in our hearts with each other. It's kinda like our official end-of-summer event."

Grace crossed her arms over her chest. "Trying to *save* me now that you know I don't believe in God?"

"No. Yes. Um, exactly." Sam shook her head, laughing. "Of course I want to save you, but that isn't for me to do. I just thought you might enjoy coming with me. Makayla will be there, and Lissi and Ava Kate, and probably more people that you know from school." She shrugged. "You won't hurt my feelings if you say no, but I wanted to invite you so you know you're very welcome."

Grace smiled. "Well, thanks. Next weekend?"

"Yeah."

"I wish I could because it sounds like fun, but we're going out of town. Camping up on Petit Jean Mountain."

"Oh, that'll be fun. We went there over the summer." Sam saw Lana entering the cafeteria. "Anyway, I just wanted to invite you. I'll see you in class."

"Yeah. Thanks."

Sam turned toward her table.

"Hey, Sam?"

She spun back around. "Yeah?"

"Keep inviting me, okay?"

Grinning big, Sam nodded. "Sure." She ran back to Makayla, her heart racing as if she'd run a marathon rather than just sprinting across the school cafeteria.

She'd planted some asparagus.

Lana ran up to them. "I can't believe she actually did it."

"What?" Sam asked. She braced herself for the news of who Aubrey had assigned the story to. At least there wouldn't be more than one or two follow-up features.

"You haven't seen today's blog post?" Lana's eyes were big and round.

Sam hadn't wanted to pour salt in her wounds, so to speak. The sting of being demoted back to writing tips from teachers that nobody would ever read still burned. "Um, no. I didn't get a chance."

And she'd also been a bit worried about needing to apologize to Makayla. Saying she was sorry *was* hard, even if it was the right thing to do.

"You have got to read it," Lana said, tugging her toward the door. Makayla followed, snatching up their backpacks.

They ran down the breezeway, ducking past the security guard into the media center. Mrs. Forge glanced up as they entered, recognized Makayla, smiled, then went back to her computer.

Busy with a game of solitaire, no doubt.

Once at the computer, Lana turned to Makayla. "I can't get to the website."

Makayla took over the keyboard. Within seconds of her fingers flying over the keys, the *Senator Speak* page loaded for them to read.

> **... It is a rare thing indeed for a middle school's newspaper reporter to not only report with diligence but also with honesty.**

The entire *Senator Speak* editorial staff is proud of our own Sam Sanderson for her breakthrough reporting of the Chenal 9 bomb incident. Sam turned over key evidence to the police to assist their investigation, and now the case is solved. Well done, Sam Sanderson. Well done. Sound Off, Senators. Leave a comment with your thoughts. ~ Luke Jensen, reporting

"Ohmygummybears!" Sam couldn't believe Aubrey had let Luke post the article, and she really couldn't believe Luke had written it in the first place.

Luke Jensen. Hello?

Mrs. Forge looked up, frowning. "You girls need to go ahead and sign off. The bell will ring in a moment."

"Before you do," Lana said, "look at how many comments you have."

Sam scrolled down to see. Four hundred and eighteen. Seriously?

All expressing congratulations to Sam and the newspaper. Even comments from Mr. Hughes and Mr. Milner. And the superintendent of the school district. Oh, and even a couple of members of the school board. Oh, oh … and Mom and Dad and Captain York …

And the editor from the high school newspaper! He'd posted: Good job on stellar reporting. Looking forward to welcoming some of the staff to the high school paper.

Oh. My. Gummy. Bears.

Editor of the Senator Speak, *here I come!*

ACKNOWLEDGEMENTS

I owe a huge amount of gratitude to my editor on this series, Kim Childress. Not just for taking interest in the project and working hard to see it come to print, but for falling in love with Sam and Makayla and the rest of the characters. Your excitement about this series feeds my excitement, and you have been awesome to work alongside. I thank you from the bottom of my heart for allowing me to share Sam and the gang with the rest of the world.

My thanks to the whole team at Zonderkidz for helping the Samantha Sanderson series see the light of day. I truly appreciate each of you for extending your talent and skill on my behalf. It's been a fun journey.

Special thanks to Robinson Middle School, who let me share how special they are with the rest of the world. I played around with possibilities and lay of the land as I saw fit. Any mistakes in the representation of details are mine, where I twisted them in the best interest of my story.

My most sincere thanks to my awesome agent, Steve Laube (HP), who not only is an amazing agent but also makes me laugh when I get too serious. THANK YOU.

My extended family members are my biggest fans and greatest cheerleaders. Thank you for ALWAYS being in my corner: Mom, BB and Robert, Bek and Krys, Bubba and Lisa, Brandon, Rachel, and Aunt Millicent. Especially my Papa, whom I love and miss every day.

I couldn't do what I do without my girls — Emily Carol, Remington Case, and Isabella Co-Ceaux. I love each of you so much! Thank y'all so much for your support and encouragement when I needed to write. And my precious grandsons, Benton and Zayden. You are joys in my life.

I'm blessed to have such an amazing husband, who not only puts up with my craziness but also is a great brainstorm partner and research assistant. You amaze me with your insight and your love and support. I love you with everything I have.

Finally, all glory to my Lord and Savior, Jesus Christ. I can do all things through Him who gives me strength.

DISCUSSION QUESTIONS

1. Sam has her mind set on her future career — to be a journalist like her mom. Do you have an idea of what career you'd like to have? Discuss different career options you're interested in.

2. Sam's dad is a policeman who is dedicated to serving and protecting his town. Do you know any police officers? Discuss how their job impacts you and your family.

3. Following the bomb threat at the theater, lots of kids were scared and unsure. How would you feel if you were one of them? What does the Bible tell us about being scared? (See Hebrews 13:6 for discussion)

4. Aubrey goes out of her way to be rude to Sam. Has someone ever treated you like that? How did you react? Discuss reasons why people act like that.

5. Makayla and Sam are both in EAST, and both very into electronic technology. Does your school have a technology program like EAST? What are some of your favorite gadgets? How do they help you learn?

6. Sam is being taught the lesson of how powerful our words can be, both written and spoken. What does the Bible say about our words? (See Proverbs 12:18)

7. Sam uses the school's paper and blog to "slant" perception of events. Discuss how the local news media might do the same in your area.

8. Because of her job, Sam's mom is out of town a lot. Does one of your parents travel a lot for their work? Discuss how it makes, or could make, you feel.

9. Sam's parents have pet names for her (pumpkin and my sweet girl) which are terms of endearment. What nicknames or pet names do you have?

10. Sam and Makayla enjoy their church's youth group and feel safe in discussing things that are on their hearts there. Everybody needs a place where they feel safe to talk about difficult subjects. What's your place?

11. Sam is a cheerleader and on the school paper. Makayla is in karate. What extracurricular activities do you enjoy? Why or why not? What would be something you'd like to try? Why?

12. If you were a student at RMS, whom would you most want to be friends with? Why?

faiThGirLz!

SAMANTHA SANDERSON

ON THE SCENE

BOOK TWO

ROBIN CARROLL

CHAPTER ONE

"Then I just felt the *pop*. Next thing I knew, I couldn't even stand up." Jefferson Cole's red hair hung over his forehead, almost reaching his blue eyes. His voice hadn't deepened like some of the other guys' at Joe T. Robinson Middle School already had.

Samantha "Sam" Sanderson glanced over the list of questions in the Notes app of her latest version iPhone. "Do you have any idea how your ankle got hurt?" she asked him. Last week, during the seventh graders' game against the Pulaski Academy Bruins, Jefferson had gotten hurt.

He shook his head. "Like I said, I was running to the end zone, was tackled, then felt my ankle snap. It took two guys to take me down. One of them landed on my leg." He lifted a single shoulder. "Coach said one of them oafs probably came down on it wrong."

"Bet it hurt."

"Like you wouldn't believe." The freckles seemed to jump off his face.

"You had to be rushed to the hospital?"

"I wouldn't say I had to be rushed to the hospital, exactly," Jefferson answered.

Sam gritted her teeth. He needed to work with her here.

It was bad enough she'd been assigned this story in the first place. Aubrey Damas, school newspaper editor and thorn in Sam's side, had given Sam this assignment, knowing full well that whoever reported anything negative about sports would have half the school upset with them.

Robinson Senators stood behind their team one hundred percent. That Sam was a cheerleader made her writing an article on the dangers of football even worse. Aubrey knew that and had given Sam the assignment on purpose.

"But you went to the hospital straight from the game, right?" Sam pushed. Having to be rushed to the hospital sounded a lot more interesting than saying that he went to the doctor and was treated for an ankle fracture. Not really blazing the journalism world with this stuff.

"Yeah. Doctor says I have to stay in this soft cast for the rest of the week." Jefferson leaned his head back against his couch. "He said I have some tendon damage, so Coach will probably bench me for the whole season just to be safe."

Talk about a flare for the dramatic. Sam turned her head so he couldn't see her grin. She glanced around the Cole's living room, noticing again the boxes piled in the corner. Oh, they were nearly hidden by the recliner, but she'd noticed them when Mrs. Cole had let Sam in. Probably Mr. Cole's things.

By now, most everyone at school knew the Coles were separated and heading toward divorce. Sam had overheard — for once, she hadn't been purposefully eavesdropping — one of the ladies at church mention that Mr. Cole had rented an apartment nearby. It was sad for a family to break up. Sam had been praying for them, especially Jefferson's sister, Nikki, who was on the newspaper staff with Sam. Nikki was Aubrey's best friend, which meant Nikki wasn't exactly friendly toward Sam.

Jefferson cleared his throat. "Dad says he'll talk with Coach after my cast is off. He told me he'd work with me every weekend to practice plays. Maybe I'll stand a chance of making the eighth grade team next year," he said. "I hope so. Man, I heard they might let some eighth graders play with the ninth graders next year, too."

"That's promising." Sam couldn't imagine being so fired up about being hit, but whatever. A lot of people didn't understand her passion to become a journalist.

Jefferson nodded. "Dad says it'll take a lot of hard work, but we can do it."

"I'm sure you'll make it." Sam didn't miss the emphasis on *we* ... was Jefferson planning on living with his dad after the big D? Nikki hadn't said anything about living arrangements. Then again, she didn't really talk to Sam. Because of Aubrey, Nikki and Sam didn't talk much. Still, Sam couldn't help feeling sorry for all of the Cole family.

"I'm studying both the seventh grade and eighth grade playbooks all the time. I nearly have everything memorized already. Dad says — "

"Who brought this in?" Nikki's voice rose above the music coming from the den where she'd been supposedly doing homework since Sam had arrived at the Cole house. She stormed into the living room, waving a piece of paper. "Jefferson, did you put this on the front door?"

Her brother tapped the top of his cast. "Seriously?"

Nikki turned her glare to Sam. "*You*. Did you do this?"

Sam started to claim innocence, but curiosity got the better of her. "Let me see." She stood and held out her hand.

Nikki thrust the paper at Sam. "You did this. You wrote this and left it at the front door, didn't you?"

Smoothing the paper, Sam read the single sentence, written in black, bold block letters:

NIKKI COLE IS A FATTY

"Why would you do something like this? Are you the one making the calls, too?" Nikki's face turned redder than Sam's shoulders had been sunburned just two weeks ago. "Why? Why would you do this? Aubrey's right — you are jealous of us."

Jealous? Of Aubrey and Nikki? Oh, puhleeze. But that wasn't the issue at the moment. "Nikki, I didn't do this. I promise. I wouldn't do such a thing." This was just mean and nasty. Sam would never stoop so low. "You've gotten calls? What kind?"

"You're going to deny it?"

Sam shook her head. "Nikki, I know we aren't friends, but you have to believe me. You know I'd never lower myself to something like this."

Nikki paused, studying Sam for a long moment, then she snatched the paper away. "Never mind. Just forget about it." She spun and stomped from the room.

Sam started to follow her.

"Don't bother." Jefferson's words stopped Sam. "She'll lock herself in her room to cry, then Mom will go talk to her for a long time before ending up calling Dad to come have dinner with us."

If he knew his sister's routine

"Has she gotten notes like that before?" Sam sunk back into her seat on the chair across from the couch. She couldn't imagine someone being so bold as to write such a hateful thing, let alone deliver it.

But Jefferson nodded.

"Just like that?"

He shrugged. "Sometimes it says she's ugly. And she's gotten a couple of text messages saying she's fat and ugly too."

Text messages meant a phone number. "Has she recognized the phone number?"

He shook his head. "Nope. Dad tried calling it back, but it just rang until he got the recording that the voice mailbox hadn't been set up yet."

"What do the police say?" Sam's dad was a detective with the Little Rock Police Department, so she put a lot of stock in law enforcement investigations.

Jefferson's eyes widened. "We haven't called the police. Calling a girl fat and ugly isn't a crime."

Now it was Sam's turn to shake her head. "This is beyond just calling someone names. Texting and writing her notes—that can be considered bullying. All states have some form of law against bullying, so it actually *is* a crime."

"I didn't know that."

"Yeah. It can become real serious." She nodded toward the doorway Nikki had left through. "You see how upset that made her. Some people get stuff like that constantly. A lot of teenagers. Until they can't take it anymore." Sam didn't want to talk about all the documentaries she'd seen about how many kids had hurt themselves or worse because of one form or another of bullying. "Your mom or dad should call the police and report it."

"I'll tell them."

Good. Maybe the police could find out who was behind this and catch them before Nikki got even more upset. In the meantime, Sam made a mental vow to pay attention to everyone around Nikki at school. "How long ago did this start?"

"Yesterday, I think." Jefferson answered.

Hmmm.

"Do you have any more questions about my injury?" Jefferson's question pulled Sam from her thoughts.

"Uh, no." She'd better get professional. If she wanted to be seen as a serious journalist like her mom, she had to act like a pro no matter how dull the assignment. She forced a smile and stood, slipping her phone into her backpack. "I think I have everything I need. Aubrey said Marcus had already come by and taken your picture?"

"He left just a few minutes before you got here."

The school paper's photographer was always on time. Sam didn't think Marcus had missed a deadline. Ever.

Neither had she, but she had the career goal to become not just a journalist but the *best*. She'd wanted to be a journalist ever since she could remember. Following in Mom's footsteps and all. Her travels ... her experiences ... Sam wanted all that for herself one day.

"Well, thanks for the interview." Sam slung her backpack over her shoulder. "I'd better get going. I'll see myself out."

"Thanks. Oh, and please don't say anything about Nikki's notes or texts. She gets mad if she thinks I've gotten into her business." Jefferson gave a weak smile.

Sam nodded. "I understand, but do talk with your mom and dad about calling the police. They have an anti-bullying department that can help. At least they could trace the number the texts came from."

"I will," Jefferson said.

Sam nodded, then let herself out the front door. Nikki only lived a couple of blocks from Sam, so she'd put off the interview until this afternoon. Her article was due tomorrow, but she wasn't worried. She didn't have any homework, so could easily write the article tonight.

Taking these less-than-awesome assignments and turning out a quality article was a right step on her career path. Great reporter this year, editor-in-chief next year. Then, hello high school paper. The only way Robinson High School's newspaper accepted a freshman on staff was if they'd been the editor of the middle school's paper.

Her mind kept as brisk a pace as her walking. Who could be sending those notes and texts to Nikki? Aside from her being Aubrey's BFF, no one had a reason not to like Nikki. Of course, there was no telling if Aubrey, and Nikki by association, might have said the wrong thing to the wrong person.

Was Aubrey getting notes and texts, too?.

The air outside was still. Sam's scalp felt hot under her long, thick hair. If she stayed out much longer, she'd be sweating.

Sam sprinted across the yard to her garage door. She punched in the code on the keypad by the door. The mechanical door opened with a creak and a squeak. Dad needed to work on that. She'd have to remember to tell him.

She raced into the house. Chewy, her German hunt terrier dog, met her at the door, jumping and wagging her whole body. Sam chuckled, then let the dog out into the backyard before starting on dinner. This morning before school, she'd pulled one of the casseroles from the freezer and shoved it into the refrigerator. That meant it wouldn't take nearly as long to cook, so it should be ready just about the time Dad would get home from work.

When Mom was home, Sam would help her make casseroles that were easy to freeze and store. That way, when Mom was off on a journalism assignment, Sam and her dad always had home-cooked meals.

Tonight was one of those nights, but Mom would be home next week.

Sam had just finished dumping the salad mix into the bowls when the front door squeaked open. Something else Dad needed to work on when he had time. His keys clanked into the wooden bowl on the entry table. "Hi, Daddy," she called out.

"Hi, pumpkin." As usual, he went immediately to his and Mom's room to lock up his gun and badge.

She added dressing and cheese to the salads, then set them on the placemats on the kitchen table.

"Something smells good." Dad kissed the top of her head as he came into the kitchen.

"It's stuffed bell pepper casserole," Sam answered as she handed him the hot pads.

"No wonder my stomach's growling." He pulled the casserole from the oven and set it on the cooling rack.

She turned off the oven and passed him the silver server and two plates. He cut generous pieces of the cheesy, meaty casserole, then carried the plates to the table. Sam joined him, carrying two glasses of milk.

Dad said grace. Her own stomach growling, Sam shoved a bite of the hot casserole into her mouth. The yummy tomato and cheese flavors made her taste buds stand up and dance. She couldn't help making a little sighing sound.

Shaking his head, Dad laughed. "You enjoy your food like your mother."

"I'll take that as a compliment," Sam answered and smiled before taking another bite.

"How was school today?"

"Good. I interviewed a football player who got hurt in last week's game. He hurt his ankle and will probably not be able to play the rest of the season."

"Ouch."

Sam nodded. "He's not really happy about it." She could kind of understand. If she couldn't cheer for a season, she'd be pretty upset. Or, if for some strange reason she couldn't be on the *Senator Speak* staff for even a week, *that* would be a fate worse than death.

"How was your day?" she asked.

"Uneventful, the way I like it." Dad smiled. It was a nice smile. Her dad was pretty handsome, if she did say so herself. Dad's hair had turned salt-and-pepper, but the pepper was still winning the race.

"You're writing a feature on this football player?" Dad asked.

She nodded. "Just one article. It's due tomorrow, but I don't have any homework." She took a sip of the cold milk. Mom only let them drink milk or water with dinner. Every now and again, Dad would let her have a soda, which was a treat, but to be honest, Sam liked milk.

"I thought you had cheer practice tonight since you have a game tomorrow." Dad wiped his mouth with the paper towel folded beside his plate.

Sam shook her head. "Mrs. Holt said we needed the break so we'd be charged and ready tomorrow for the pep rally."

"Makes sense."

She just couldn't stop thinking about Nikki's notes and texts. "Hey, Dad …"

"Yes?"

"What are the laws about bullying here?"

"Why? Are you being bullied?" Dad's face turned into his *bulldog* look — eyebrows drawn down, lips puckered tight. His cheeks even seemed to sink in.

"No, not me. Just someone I know." She finished off her milk, but her mouth still felt like it was stuffed with cotton balls.

"Sam, if you know someone's being bullied, you have to report it."

"She told her parents. I'm sure they're handling it." Well, maybe. Maybe Jefferson told Mr. and Mrs. Cole they needed to contact the police, if not the school.

Dad didn't release his bulldog expression. "Bullying is very serious, Sam. That's why there are laws to protect kids from being bullied. Here in Arkansas, bullying is a class B misdemeanor. People convicted of bullying, and that includes cyber-bullying, face up to ninety days in jail and fines up to a thousand dollars."

"Oh, I know it's serious." But she'd have thought the punishment would be more than just a couple of months in jail and having to pay less than a thousand bucks.

"You should encourage your friend to make sure her parents not only tell Mrs. Trees and other school administrators but also the police."

The principal of the middle school, Mrs. Trees, had zero tolerance for any type of misbehaving. Sam had no doubt she wouldn't allow any type of bullying to go on in her school.

"Let me know if you'd like me to speak to her parents," Dad said.

Nikki would flip her lid and Sam would really be socially outcast then.

"I'll let you know. Thanks, Dad."

Even though she had no plans of telling Dad who was being bullied, Sam had every intention of finding out who was behind it.

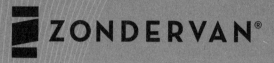

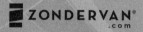